THE LAST
COLD-WAR
COWBOY

JAMES PARK SLOANE

THE LAST COLD-WAR COWBOY

A Critic's Choice paperback
from Lorevan Publishing, Inc.
New York, New York

Reprinted by arrangement with William Morrow and Co., Inc.

ISBN: 1-55547-252-4

First Critic's Choice edition: 1988

From LOREVAN PUBLISHING, INC.

Critic's Choice Paperbacks
31 E. 28th St.
New York, New York 10016

Manufactured in the United States of America

For Eugene and Anna, whose young lives set forth a standard for excellence; and for sustaining friends—Giorgio and Graziella, Dominick and Kathleen, Peter, and Jeanette.

"And ye shall know the truth and the truth shall make you free."
—Carved in marble in the lobby of CIA headquarters, Langley, Virginia

"The crocodile is quick to sink but slow to come up."
—Indonesian proverb

THE LAST COLD-WAR COWBOY

Undated Draft
Copy <u>1</u> of <u>2</u> copies
TO: DDCI
FROM: - DIR
SUBJECT: Damage Assessment
-- CABBAGE

THIS REPORT AND ALL
PAGES GRADED TS EYES
ONLY DDCI, DCI, DIR
  DO NOT DETACH
  DO NOT COPY
  DO NOT CROSS REF

SUMMARY AND RECOMMENDATIONS

1. Case officer code named CABBAGE, currently in Libya, is regarded as a defector. Notice posted to sections.

2. Assistance is being rendered to ODYOKE agencies seeking to apprehend subject and/or recover assets within U.S. jurisdiction.

3. The following operations should be regarded as compromised in whole or in part:

> Italy, 1948
> Burma, 1950
> Tehran, 1953
> Manila, 1954

Vietnam, 1957
Sumatra, 1958
Congo, 1961
Libya, 1969

Congo is coded D-1 and Libya is coded B-2 (references appended). KUCAGE has been charged with preparation of fallback disinformation to be disseminated as required.

4. The office of the IG has been charged with responsibility for conducting internal review of actions undertaken by CABBAGE on his own initiative and without KUDOVE authority. Report due 90 days from the above date.

5. Current operations compromised: none.

6. Subject had limited access to weapons development and communications programs under KUBARK Directive 2138-PP. Level of compromise remains subject to ongoing evaluation by DIR.

7. Public dissemination of information and any further liaison with ODACID or other ODYOKE agencies should be at the exclusive discretion of the DCI.

8. This file to be reviewed monthly until one year after the above date and semiannually thereafter. All copies to be destroyed under DCI-101 one year after final disposition.

JPT/DIR
initialed

Then.

Prologue: **Coup**

Jakarta is just like any other city in the dead irons of the night. You wonder how they can afford to let all that physical plant sit idle while interest accrues on the national debt. Some people can't.

You want to picture Jakarta, you picture those grainy 1950s newsreels of hard-eyed soldiers in pith helmets. You picture victory parades of scruffy rag-tag revolutionaries down wide dirt boulevards in any out-of-the-way Asian capital. Hanoi. Pyongyang. That's how I picture it anyway.

Now picture vans racing down those boulevards in the middle of the night. They came for the generals about three A.M. Hauled them out of bed and drove them to Halim, where the Communist Women were waiting.

They asked me a question about it on my orals. "Explain it. Explain September thirtieth, 1965."

Human nature, I was tempted to say.

"The Gestapu coup, so called," I began. "Gerulan September Tigapuluh. The 30 September Movement. I wrote a paper about it. . . ." That was all I got out before Danauer gave me a look that would have wilted bamboo. Danauer was my adviser. "If you want, I'll review the literature," I backtracked. "There's Anderson and McVey, the famous Cornell Paper. Then there's Dake, Crouch, Pauker, Roeder, May."*

"You might begin with an overview," Danauer suggested with a nod toward Frazier. Frazier was in quantitative methods and thought Indonesia was one of those dots in the South Pacific where with luck you could still find women who hadn't learned to charge for casual sex.

"The army and the PKI† were trying to get at each other while Sukarno pretended to be above the fray," I addressed myself to Frazier. "In fact, Sukarno was packing the cabinet with Communists. The Chinese were arming a People's Militia, and Subandrio was spending half his time in Peking."

Frazier's brow resolved into Lowell Thomas furrows. "Subandrio?"

"The foreign minister," I filled him in. "Sukarno was president."

"Ah, then. It's perfectly simple," Frazier said.

"The names are confusing," I granted. "You see, many Indonesian names begin with S-U. It's like Scottish names beginning with M-C or M-A-C. In Dutch script it's written S-O-E."

*See Appendix A, p. 267.
†Partai Komunis Indonesia, at that time the third largest Communist party in the world, after China and the Soviet Union

"Perfectly simple," Frazier repeated. "So the Commies got ambitious and murdered a bunch of generals."

I nodded. If Frazier wanted to take the whole exam, it was perfectly all right with me.

"The Communist Women were waiting at Halim Air Base, at a place called Lubang Pruaja. The Crocodile Hole. They were dancing and chanting. Some accounts say they were high on drugs. It was a pretty grim scene. They set upon the generals with stones and knives. Anyway, there was gouging of eyes and mutilation of sexual parts. They threw the bodies down a well."

‧ "What happened then?" Frazier wanted to know. He was really getting into it.

"A Lieutenant Colonel Untung came over the radio and announced a coup. Sukarno and Subandrio were with him at Halim. Also the air force chief of staff. Also Aidit, the head of the PKI."

"Let's get back to the role of the People's Republic," Mirsky said. He was the resident Sinologist and was just back from a sabbatical in Taipei.

"Why don't we let Mr. McCallum finish his overview, Chet," Danauer gently chided.

"It was a pivotal moment," I went on. "The coup failed. The Communists were booted out—the Chinese along with them. The American oil companies were invited back in."

"Failed?" Frazier said. "Failed why?"

"Suharto," I said. "They forgot to kill Suharto."

"I thought it was Sukarno," Frazier said.

"Sukarno was president," Danauer said without inflection. "Suharto was a general."

"And S-U-B-A-N-D-R-I-O was foreign minister," Frazier said carefully. If he wasn't careful, they were going to award him another doctorate.

"Suharto did end up as president," I said. Danauer winced.

"It's perfectly simple," Frazier said.

"It's the names that make it confusing," I said.

"It's a damn Marx Brothers routine," Frazier allowed.

"Why don't you tell us how Suharto happened to prevail," Mirsky prodded.

Danauer shot me a quick glance.

"Suharto had the Strategic Army Reserve," I said. "He got control of the palace and radio station. Then he marched on Halim. He clobbered the Gestapu people and exhumed the bodies. The coup fell apart."*

"Yes? And?" Danauer nodded me along like a catechism teacher.

"It took Suharto two years to finish off Sukarno. The first thing he did was deal with the PKI. He sent his troops out into the countryside." I stole a look at Danauer, who was nodding cautiously. "They call it the amok time. *Amok,* incidentally, is the only Indonesian word in common English usage. It means 'wild,' 'out of control.' " I was getting it. Danauer had a Red-Auerbach-up-by-nineteen-with-four-to-play look. I mean he was about to light the cigar. For the first time I began to believe that I might actually pass.

"The soldiers ran amok. They issued machetes

*See Appendix B, p. 271.

to the Muslims. Anybody who had a red card was fair game." I was coasting downhill now. "They executed entire villages. On Bali groups of Hindu Communists put on death robes to walk into the machine-gun fire. People who had no political views at all were killed by neighbors who bore personal grudges. When it was all over, journalists put the death toll at upward of half a million."

It was in the bag. Danauer's face was complete satisfaction. I had offended no one and stepped on nobody's pet theory of the world. Above all, I had maintained a controlled and measured tone. Half a million is not an insignificant number, but neither did I wish to appear overly impressed by it. This is the century of the Armenians and Ukrainians and European Jews. You don't want to get carried away by half a million dead Indonesians, but neither should you neglect the fact that in some centuries it would have made a pretty respectable massacre.

Now.

1.
Crockett

Crockett called on December 8. I remember distinctly because it was the second unexpected call in twenty-four hours. Jeremy had called the night before. He wanted to remind me that *Tora! Tora! Tora!* was on TV. He didn't want me to miss it.

I remembered when we used to watch it together. We would make popcorn, and I would do the Roosevelt speech. I do a pretty good Roosevelt. I hit the *infamy* hard, with three spondees, and I really nail the second syllable of *dastardly*. I also know how to roll the air and naval forces of the Empire of Japan from the back of the throat.

"The day your mother sees the phone bill is a day that will live in infamy," I said.

"She never bothers to check," Jeremy said. "By the time the bill comes, she'll think she made the call. Climb Mount *Niitaka*."

I promised to catch the flick. Actually I was busy doing a little article on the Tokyo Agreements, but I couldn't seem to get back into it. I flicked on the TV and caught the second half of *Tora!* and the first half of *Midway,* which was the Late Show on the same channel. It was a very patriotic channel.

About two A.M. a canned announcement came on and said that the second half of *Midway* would be shown the following evening. Until then there would be no way for a fellow to be sure that Spruance's search planes would locate the Japanese carriers. I looked it up, and sure enough, *TV Guide* said *Midway,* Part I. Just the same, it was a dastardly trick.

My friend Sorel has this theory that low moments in life, when all is dull and blah, are the times to buy. It's a nice theory if you happen to need cheering up at three o'clock in the morning. To illustrate, Sorel cites the odd fifteen-minute lull in his own colorful existence. Which is great for Sorel. I'm just not sure my life works like Advanced Micro Devices.

Crockett called the next morning at nine. I was sitting at my desk thinking about a blip on Sukarno's kidney. Honest to God I was. Crockett had it on good authority that I was the bull-goose expert on Indonesian oil and mineral policy. Could I come down to Dallas and discuss a project with him? A fee was mentioned. Could I be there tomorrow afternoon?

Dallas is such an unexpected city out in the middle of all that nothing, you wonder if Johnny A. accidentally dropped a packet of skyscraper seed.

Crockett's office was in one of those skyscrapers with a lot of black glass and a slanted roof to let you know it was built by one of the hotshots. I wondered how they could fit an office into that bevel of slanted glass, and wouldn't you know it, I was destined to find out.

On the way up in the elevator I just folded my arms and stared down at everybody's custom-made boots. There was plenty of space on the top floor, so I guess the angle is just an optical illusion. Everything in Crockett's office had that elusive European designer quality, along with a discreet little MC that you hardly knew was there but which was bound to wreck the resale value. It all made me extremely aware of the fact that the main thing I had acquired in life was about twenty-billion bits of arcane information.

"Welcome to Dallas," Crockett said. "You like the view?"

"It reminds me of what Satan showed Jesus," I said.

"Have a seat, Professor," Crockett said. "Do you have a current visa for Indonesia?"

"I can get one," I said.

"Excellent, excellent," he said, as if we had dispensed with the central difficulty right off the bat. "Tell me about the head boy over there."

I gave him the five-minute summary that Reagan gets, but without charts. Basically it said that Suharto was in control.

"Who's the opposition?"

"Muslim extremists," I said. "Suharto is a Muslim, but not a fanatic."

"How about the Reds?"

"Hard to tell," I said. "They had a big rebuilding job after 1965."

"Tell me about these overtures to North Korea."

I scanned Crockett's face. Either somebody had planted the question, or he wasn't half the ignoramus he was at pains to let on he was.

"The Indonesians have a bad case of paranoia about China," I said. "The feelers to North Korea have more to do with that than with us."

The kind of stuff I knew off the top was really astonishing. Why couldn't I get respect from Laura Westin? Crockett mulled this new information over, and I began to think more highly of the chances of turning some of my arcane knowledge into nice cuff links. "Who's the bull-goose honcho in their oil ministry?" Crockett finally said.

"Subroto," I said. "He's OPEC chairman this year, so day-to-day operations are being run by an economist named Moko."

"A reasonable fellow?"

"Always when I've been with him. We were on a panel together. His degree is from The Hague."

"That's nice," Crockett said. "My pappy always said, you don't know dogs, take the one with the pedigree."

Crockett leaned across the desk and looked me straight in the eye. It is a gesture typical of American businessmen who are about to come to the pitch.

"Now, Professor, I have shareholders and bankers to consider," he began. I could feel a speech coming about how tough life was. "It wouldn't do to put on a large piece of business over there if the head boys turned out to lack a proper respect for private property. Your friend Brother Moko was strictly reading Adam Smith, I take it?"

"No problem," I said.

Crockett sat back in his chair again. It is a gesture typical of American businessmen who have just received the right response. "I want you to go back to Chicago and write it up," he said. "How Suharto is in control, degrees from The Hague, all that. Let's say fifty pages. Throw in some charts and graphs, bankers like that shit, and be sure to mention the North Korea stuff. Get yourself a visa. When I'm done showing your report around, I have a little negotiation I want you to carry out with Brother Moko."

I said I would do what he wanted. He was so pleased that he told me what it was all about. "There's this little company called Indoil. They went hog-wild buying up Indonesian offshore tracts. It seemed smart at the time. Saudi light was going for thirty-four dollars. Of course the little tan boys insisted on fixed lifting schedules. Now Saudi light is twenty-five dollars and falling. It's a disaster. Still, there is no disaster so terrible that someone cannot find good in it."

"I take it you have found the silver lining," I said.

"Oh, yes," he said. "If you figure crude in the ground is worth at least five dollars a barrel, Indoil stock is now selling at thirty cents on the dollar. Where your friend Moko comes in is that the little tan boys are going to have to let me take my own good time sucking it up."

"Why will they do that?" I was truly curious.

"Because the little tan boys did the first thing

people do when they get smart. They got too smart. They killed the goose. Oh, they negotiated rings around the boys at Indoil, but Indoil is now a dead bird. Kaput, Chapter Eleven inside of twelve months. I can't picture American courts sucking up oil at a loss for the benefit of the Indonesian current account, can you?" Crockett wiggled himself comfortably into the back of his chair the way a man does when the world confirms his views. "The only real trick is to get out there and get the goodies before that bastard Boone Pickens beats me to it."

Crockett reached into his desk and came out with two cigars. They were large and packed in miniature Minuteman missiles and required preparation by a lethal-looking tool that Crockett used as a paperweight. The one Crockett handed across to me had a dryish smell, and I could tell that it had almost nothing in common with the Antonio y Cleopatras I had affected as a graduate student. Crockett snipped the end off both cigars and lit mine with his Saarinen cigarette lighter. It was then that I noticed the logo on his orange and black tie. He was a Princeton man.

When I got to the airport, Crockett's dogsbody made them upgrade my ticket. It was the moment in the movie when Young Jimmy Kildare is made aware that there are possibilities in life other than pure research. One of the pleasures of doing business with Crockett was that it was first class all the way. It's so well worth it on a corporate budget when Sam is picking up 50 percent. A university just doesn't feel right spending money that way, not even if it happens to be located in Texas. I had just about persuaded myself that the North Korea question had been planted by one of his backers, who had probably gotten it out of the *Sunday Times*.

It was an additional reason for taking notice, though, when the fall copy of *Pacifica* turned up in the open briefcase of one of the businicrats in the last row of the first-class section. I caught just a glimpse of it on the way back from nature's call. It's amazing, really, how little of the cover you have to see to recognize a magazine in which you yourself have an article. I told myself it was just the kind of little anomaly a person has to get used to when the world finally begins to fall to his true capacities.

2.
Insomnia

The paper was easily the best thing written on the coup, and never mind that it was written fifteen years ago for Danauer's graduate seminar. Never mind, either, that it attacked every senior scholar in the field. Danauer had given it an A− during the era when an A of any sort from Danauer was like being doused with a vial of anointing oil. The minus was just Danauer's way of reminding one that all scholarly judgments are subject to qualification.

I suppose it could have used a qualification or two, although that is not the sort of thing that occurs to a second-year graduate student at four o'clock in the morning. "Audacious and cleverly reasoned, if impertinent and overly dogmatic for work drawn entirely from secondary sources" went Danauer's brief comment. "See me in office hours." And all I had said was that Anderson, McVey, Dake, Crouch, Pauker, Roeder, and May were all full of it up to their ears.

"Couldn't you find someone else to offend?" Danauer said at office hours. "Or perhaps for that you would require access to primary sources."

"I didn't exactly say they were wrong," I countered.

"Only that their views were contradictory, and that no interpretation of the coup could be supported on the available data. And you implied . . ."

"But is it publishable?"

"Publishable?" Danauer rolled the thought around in guttural consonants. "In *Ramparts,* perhaps. Publish," he echoed Wellington, "and drive taxis."

I was two thirds of the way to my doctorate, and Danauer had already as much as agreed to be my thesis adviser. I got the message. The paper went to the bottom of my file drawer, where it lay for fifteen years. Until insomnia rooted it out.

Don't think I don't appreciate insomnia. Properly used, it can add up to 30 percent to a man's productive life. It's quality of life that worries me. With insomnia you tend not to live your life all the way up.

It started about a year ago and got a second wind last spring when Helen flew the coop. I mentioned it to Sorel. Helen had always insisted that Sorel was a gangster, but in point of fact he runs a commodities and options firm with seats on both the MERC and the CBOT. Sorel and I play racquetball every Tuesday and Thursday at seven A.M. Sorel is convinced that nothing can go wrong in life that can't be fixed by a sauna, a cold beer, and a poker game.

"Hit back at it," he said. "Show it who's boss. If you're gonna be awake, make constructive use of your time."

What Sorel suggested was that I join his Friday night poker game. He said it would do me good. I should have known better. I spent two hours in the Regenstein boning up on the rules so as not to embarrass him in front of his friends. By evening I was in full command of the fact that a royal flush beats a full house and that one is advised against drawing into an inside straight. I even had a rudimentary sense of how you go about calculating the odds. Around midnight I won my first hand and the whole table applauded. I won another one around two A.M. By three A.M. I was $179 down and beginning to consider the use of toothpicks to prop my eyelids open. I thanked Sorel for a lovely diversion and tried to keep my eyes open to the point on the expressway from which the car knows the way.

I slept about ten minutes. The garage door was banging at an irregular interval. The neighbor's cat was enjoying the latter stages of a successful seduction. I got up and walked past the room which had been Jeremy's, and which will be his still if I don't sell the house before summer. I flicked the light on and off and walked on down to my study.

It's easy for people like Sorel to say you should just get up and work. The walls of my study are lined with books, half of which Jeremy had thoughtfully alphabetized. Have you ever tried to find an anthology by three obscure editors among two thousand half-alphabetized books at four o'clock in the morning?

I decided to go through my files instead. My files consist of about fifteen large cardboard boxes. The system is strictly LIFO. Whatever I kept from yesterday's mail is on top. I started with the fourteenth box, which seemed as good a place as any. The item on top was a syllabus I first put together in 1973. There were grade rosters with the forgotten names of students who were now married, divorced, separated, having love affairs, and suffering their first heart attacks. There were a number of Jeremy's early paintings, from before verisimilitude became a factor, and some old love letters Helen had written during our courtship. The paper was the second item from the bottom.

That was some time in April. My neighbor's cat is getting up in years, and he doesn't get up to much when the temperature at midnight is in excess of fifty-five degrees. I had the garage door fixed in late May when the Sears repairman got back from an off-season trip to Barbados.

All those years in the bottom of my files hadn't changed the paper a bit. Time had not withered it, and custom never had a chance. It didn't even have typos, which spoke well, I thought, for a grad student of that era. I retyped the title page to get rid of the date and the last page to get rid of Danauer's comment, and, oh, yes, I added a couple of recent articles to the bibliography; then I mailed it off before second thoughts could set in.

Pacifica took it, a little grudgingly I thought. At forty, I am a full professor at a major university with two published books,* one of them the standard work in the field, so *Pacifica* could hardly say no. I know, I know. Danauer had warned me. The sun and stars were going to fall; I would wreck my career and ruin my life. He had even arranged a grant for me to do statistical research in Jakarta like Old Dr. Gillespie saving Young Jimmy Kildare from his damfool notions. But that was fifteen years ago, and Danauer had retired. When the galleys arrived for proofing, the sun and stars were still in their appointed places. The only trouble was that I still wasn't sleeping.

NOTA BENE: Insomnia has a clairvoyant way about it. When you are about to make a costly mistake, insomnia knows. (It is also informed well in advance when your wife is about to run off with an English professor.) Sorel has a theory about it, of course, to wit: Insomnia is a leading indicator. You don't get insomnia because of the bad things that have happened to you, you get insomnia because of the bad things that are *going* to happen to you.

The first warning sign was when San Diego suddenly turned lukewarm about a guest lecture. The second was when I wasn't asked to run a panel at the Hawaii Conference. The third was when Gus Friedler managed to avoid me at every low dive in Honolulu. Gus and I had been in grad school at the same time, and we had cross-referenced each other's work until we became close friends. What Gus was avoiding having to say was that IRCA,† of which he was a board member, had already decided to turn down my grant application.

*See Appendix C, p. 273.
†International Relations Council, Asian Division

I told myself it wasn't a catastrophe. I had a SEAAAC* grant already on the books, which included travel money for my work on the Tokyo Agreements. I could live with a slow period. The trouble was, insomnia wasn't done with me yet. It had been conducting a systematic review of my character defects. I am an indifferent friend, and a worse husband. My Little League coach had accused me of having a bad attitude and being self-centered. I hadn't visited my mother in two years or written my college roommate in more than five. I have a bad record for returning phone calls. I had promised Gran on her deathbed to become a minister. Well, not promised exactly. I had hedged my statement pretty carefully and kept my fingers crossed, and it is unclear whether promises made under duress are binding anyway. But I had insinuated. My personal judgments are often unsound. I always vote for the loser in presidential elections and invariably buy stocks the day before the release of unexpected bad news. God probably exists.

The *Pacifica* article was in my hands by the first of November. It was such a small dull thing, and yet the raveled-sleeve knitter ever eluded me. My life was changing. Millionaires valued my opinions while old friends avoided me in bars. I flew first class on airplanes, where businessmen brought along my work for casual reading. One more significant event and I was going to become a high-risk heart-attack candidate.

I woke up on December 10 with an uneasy feel-

*Southeast Asian Affairs Advisory Council

ing. It was just possible that totally by chance a person carrying an obscure journal with an article I had written was sitting three rows behind me on the Dallas-Chicago flight. C. G. Jung believed in that sort of thing. He called it synchronicity. Personally, I am a skeptic. I wished I had been rude enough to stare and figure out which of the three men in the back row went with the briefcase.

That was one thing. The other thing was that I had slept a net three hours, and though they say that lying flat on your back is 90 percent as good, I don't believe them for one minute. As if that wasn't enough, my neighbor had chosen this morning to block the driveway. My neighbor and I share the driveway, which is inevitable for two houses on a block like ours. It's like being seated next to the left-hander at a dinner party. If you are already tired, and have an uneasy feeling, and are late for racquetball, it can be annoying. The thing was, he was determined to talk to me.

"So tell me your news," he said. I thought he had let his Mercedes idle a long time. A Mercedes is not supposed to have to warm up like that.

"Come again?"

"You know what I mean. I mean, you don't have to be coy with me. I don't go on talk shows. I know how to keep my mouth shut. Nobody ever asks me about anything. Except."

"I really don't know what you're talking about," I said. I really didn't.

"I mean your professional news," he said.

"Well, I'm working on this article about the Tokyo Oil Agreements of 1963. You see, Sukarno had a change of heart and decided to let the American oil companies stay; then he changed his mind again and tried to kick them out. It's really.very interesting."

My neighbor made a medicine face.

"I'm doing a little consulting work for an oil company," I said. "Also, I recently published an article on the Indonesian coup of 1965. The funny thing is, I wrote it fifteen years ago, when I was a graduate student. You see, a group of generals was murdered . . ."

I could just tell he wasn't really interested.

"Be that way, then," he said. "But I know what's what. G-men don't come around asking questions about guys who write oil articles. Big shot."

His face had a hurt look that was only partially faked. He gunned the poor Mercedes and bumped it over the curb. Helen had been telling him for years that we ought to go together and widen that driveway. A Mercedes just isn't meant for that sort of thing.

3.
Mandala

It threw me right off my racquetball game. I lost the first to Sorel in about ten minutes and was down two points in the second. There were a lot of long rallies, though, and to catch his breath Sorel asked if I had something on my mind. I told him about the *Pacifica* article and the men who had talked to my neighbor.

"You ever do any work for one of the spook agencies?"

Sorel had a way of cutting to the heart of things. It was also one of those adroitly phrased questions where a flat no wouldn't pass a polygraph. "Sort of," I said.

I won six of the next seven points, three of them on reverse corners. "A fellow named Oren Lewes remembered me from Vietnam," I said in between jerking him around the court. "Lewes grew up to run the

Far East desk at DDA.* One day he runs across my name in a scholarly journal. He flies me to Washington, takes me for lunch at Blackie's and drinks at Teddy's, commends my patriotism, and signs me up to write a report on Malaysian tin smuggling."

"You had to have a security clearance for that?" Sorel asked. He was leaning against the side wall after chasing a nick. I was on a roll. It was one of those adrenaline highs you sometimes get on three hours' sleep.

"Already had one, from the army," I said. I would have liked to play another couple of points before his heart rate got down. Sorel is one of those heavy suety guys who gets winded but recovers really quick. When he kept stalling, it meant I had him on the run.

"Renewing my clearance was pro forma. The stuff on tin was low level, but it was going into a report with an overall TS. Bureaucratic brain damage."

Sorel played two points without asking a question and split them on a lucky back-wall rebound. "So they parachute you into the the jungle with knife, cyanide, and gold bracelets."

"I got it from Professor Panjang in Kuala Lumpur. He's a tin expert." With all this explaining, I was starting to huff and puff myself. "Coolies smuggle the tin down to Singapore on bicycles. The big money is made by a couple of Singapore Chinese and the Malaysian connection in Penang. The Malay end of it is Panjang's black-sheep brother."

"I see," Sorel said. "In the future, you get any fresh info on developments in that market, you come

*Deputy Directorate for Analysis. See Appendix D, p. 274.

straight to Brother Sorel. Brother Sorel is in the way of knowing how to insert dollars into the tin market."

I promised I would. The long sentence had been a dead giveaway. I really had him now. He was huffing and puffing like a slow freight train. I served an ace that he hardly moved for, and he asked me how the DDA thing turned out.

"Oh, they loved me at DDA. Then about six months later Panjang came up to me at the Manila Conference, and he was madder than hell. A covert type from the embassy had tried to recruit him. Threatened to expose his brother unless Panjang forked over cabinet minutes. Panjang worked in the Ministry of Finance."

"And?" I had him in the corner again, but he threw back a pretty good lob.

"Panjang told the spook where to shove it. He offered to resign, but Malays are a forgiving sort. They're short of first-rate economists, too."

"I didn't realize you were in the army," Sorel said. He had won the lob point, but it cost him a lot of oxygen. His sentences didn't, though.

"Army Intelligence," I said. I was holding my own.

"Nam?"

"We called it Vietnam." I got carried away. "I was a district intelligence adviser. After I had a mo-. torcycle accident they sent me to Saigon. That's where I'm supposed to have met Oren Lewes."

"Lewes?"

"The guy who hired me at DDA." Sorel was really being brazen about this. "In Saigon he worked for Bill Colby."

"Operation Phoenix!" Sorel blurted. He cut loose

with a back-wall ricochet that caught me entirely off balance.

"You got it," I said. "I was in it. I learned all about it five years later at a dinner party."

"They have you knocking off VC organizers?"

"I used to haul pouches from MACJ-2* to the CIA reception desk. They wanted to make me a typist, but I was overqualified. A lieutenant with a broken arm and TS Crypto clearance was a big-enough investment to serve as courier. That's where Lewes said he noticed me."

"Must have been better-looking then," Sorel said. He unleashed a terrific drive along the right wall. I mean, he really got his weight into it. He was starting to creep up on me. "So what did you do?"

"About Phoenix? Nothing."

"About the report, asshole. Your friend Wang Hung."

I generally ignore Sorel's attempts at humor. "Called Lewes and raised holy hell. He flew me to Washington to explain that it was a mistake. More drinks at Teddy's. Profuse apologies. I declined renewal just the same. It wasn't worth a friendship."

Sorel nodded. While I was talking he had crept up and pulled dead even. He was really surging now. He won one on a little feathery drop shot, then nailed a backhand into the corner, which didn't come up for game and match. "That's the only thing of real value in life," he said thoughtfully.

"What's that?" I said.

"Good inside information," Sorel said.

*Military Assistance Command, Vietnam, Joint Staff (Intelligence)

Sorel told me not to worry. It sounded to him like a Chinaman* was looking after my interests. It was probably a job offer, and I would hear from it in the near future. It made me feel better as far as the locker-room door. Invisible hands pulling the strings in my life had always been a negative indicator. I kept thinking about it on the drive to work.

It was just like me not to have known about a thing like Operation Phoenix. I had caught my Vietnamese counterpart, Dai Uy Han, torturing prisoners and turned him in. MACJ-2 in Saigon cabled back a request for full details, the subtext of which was WHAT ARE YOU CRAZY? It never made any sense to me until that dinner party. The dean's wife started going on about Operation Phoenix. She had read about it in the *Times*, and they had discussed it at her church. The atrocities bothered her a lot. Helen was quick to mention that I had been there.

Had I seen an atrocity? Had I indeed. I had managed to put a stop to one for about three weeks until I had a motorcycle accident on a back road on the way to get my ashes hauled. It was the way things worked in my life. The motorcycle I had the accident on I had won in a poker game (pairs and three of a kind—that should have made me suspicious). I had been two hundred dollars up and this ETSing† buck sergeant said if I would throw in another two in cash American dollars I could have the bike. While we were still friends Dai Uy Han assured

*In certain business and intelligence circles, slang for sponsor
†Estimated Termination of Service, used as a verb by Vietnam Era soldiers about to go home

me the bike had a pre-accident black-market value of at least one hundred dollars.

The girl I rode the bike to visit was a Chinese-Vietnamese named Xuan who had a small Eurasian boy who she said belonged to her sister in Saigon (they all do, they all do). The MACJ-2 computer (I put her through an Agency-Check-Plus basis her agent potential) said every word she uttered had been true except that the kid was sponsored by an AID adviser who had ETSed three years previous. I couldn't help wondering who tipped the VC with the high-tension wire that continued to hold my attention while the motorbike caromed forty or fifty meters down the road.

People are always spinning webs around me. What did I do? I can still see the poor VC cadreman strapped into what looked like a used electric chair while Day Uy Han satisfied his curiosity about the infrastructure. If you've seen a man tortured, you don't forget it. It's like eating puffer fish or skiing the glacier at Courmayeur. It has texture. You put yourself right into the scene. You see what human beings are made of. It's called protoplasm, and awful things can be done to it.

I rolled into the parking garage, managed not to go over the spikes in the wrong direction, inserted my card properly on the second try, and walked to my office. I was doing my best to get my mind back on the Tokyo Agreements. I *was* interested in them. I really was. I was interested in the fact that about that time a team of Chinese doctors had discovered a blip on Sukarno's kidney. It was supposed to help explain everything from the oil negotiations to the coup. It was the Cleopatra's nose of Indonesian politics. I had even called my own internist to ask about the state of kidney disease diagnosis and treatment in 1963, which he answered in a perfectly calm voice before inquiring whether I intended to have a retroactive case.

What you have to remember is that Indonesians have a different sense of causation from Westerners. They see the world as a mandala. It has an inside called the *lair* and an outside called the *batin*. The lair and the batin come together in a man's *kasekten*. If you have a lot of it, your face sort of glows, you are going to be terrific in bed, make tons of money and father armies. If a leader has it, his people are going to do all of the above, plus the weather is going to be balmy.

I have never understood why they have to get the blueprint for campus high-rises out of Kafka. Half the reason you get into it anyway is for the high fireplaces and seedy Persian rugs. It's hard to get into a scholarly frame of mind when you are sitting in the middle of a thirty-story slab of concrete. You just don't feel like a real professor. I don't even smoke a pipe, and I have sort of moved away from tweed jackets with patches on the sleeves, so what else do I have?

Westin was blocking the door to the faculty mail room. Laura Westin is the departmental secretary, and has been for twenty-two years. There was a Mr. Westin once, but not since Westin worked for the university. She is fifty-one, goes to Nautilus for the noon aerobics class, and has pictures of cats on the walls of her office.

"So what are they after you for?"

Somewhere under those roll-down socks I suspected there were ankles, and I also had my suspicions that those Rosie the Riveter dresses concealed a fairly decent pair of thighs.

"I beg your pardon," I said. I had known people like Westin in the army, and several of them were sergeant majors. She was really not going to let me through the door.

"I hadn't seen a haircut like that in twenty years. I tell you, it was the real McCoy. Straight from Ike and pre-rock and roll. Those boys have access to a real barber."

"You got your hair done yourself," I said. "It's very nice. What boys are these?"

"The boys who came poking around about your bad habits," Westin said. "There were two of them."

"Oh, those boys."

Westin had decided they must work for one of the really hard-core collection agencies. She told them to buzz off. She didn't give two hoots for their ID shields, which were just little pieces of metal anyone could have made up. She just knew the State Department wasn't about to hire me.

"The State Department, was it?"

But I had a feeling she was right. I was enough of a sixties child not to like people in crewcuts snooping around asking questions about my personal habits. It was bad lair being confirmed by very suspicious batin. When you lose kasekten, you see, your face doesn't glow anymore. You get blips on your kidney, volcanoes erupt, you can't sleep nights, and your generals plot against you. When Sukarno lost it, Mount Agung proceeded to erupt, confirming that he was in real trouble. You can scoff all you want, but I should have paid closer attention to the eruption of Mount Saint Helens. You have to watch these things.

4.
Angles

Westin waylaid me again after class. "Mr. Sorel called," she said. "He says he can't be reached by phone during trading hours. He would like you to drop by his office on the floor of the Mercantile Exchange."

"Thanks," I said.

"Well?"

"Well what?"

"Well you know what I mean."

"I don't know what you mean at all," I said.

"Mr. Sorel indicated in passing that you have become a close collaborator of Mr. Marlon Crockett. So give. Tell all."

"Mr. Sorel apparently operated under the erroneous assumption that you were my personal secretary," I riposted. "I am not at liberty to discuss Mr. Crockett's business. We corporate barracudas are a secretive lot. Think of the Union Corse. All I can say is, buy Indoil."

"What's Indoil?" She was already jotting it down on a departmental memo pad.

"Indoil is the old Indonesian-American Oil Partnership," I said. "Ten years ago they broke it off from the parent companies and made it a company of its own. Don't tell anybody, but Crockett is going to make a bid for it."

"The Street believes that Mr. Crockett is making a bid for Tidelands," Westin snapped.

"The Street? Tidelands?"

"Wall Street, silly. I know all about your Mr. Crockett from reading *The Wall Street Journal*," she crowed. "Tidelands is a medium-size oil producer. The risk arbs are heavily into it." I could tell she was enjoying this, she was really getting into it. "Your Mr. Crockett is supposed to be about to bid thirty-five or forty a share. It's going to be a formal tender offer for controlling shares. That's what the Street thinks."

"Then the *Street* will be the last to know," I crowed right back.

"Are you putting money into Indoil?" she wanted to know.

"Just as fast as I can get my broker on the phone," I said.

Westin mulled this over. I managed to disengage my eyes from the top of her blouse. Starching a blouse that way is just a trick to maximize assets, as they learn in junior high. It has the allure of improbability.

"How certain is all this?" She was deep in concentration.

"I have it from the mouth of the horse."

"What could go wrong?"

"Markets move in both directions." I could play this game too. "It's an uncertain world. The big boys know how to handle risk. That's how we sharks make our pile."

I was enjoying this thoroughly. Westin was the first person on the university payroll to reduce taxable income with a 403B and the first to put zero coupons in her IRA. I had once had to stand and listen while she gave me a twenty-minute lecture on the implications of tax-free compound interest, and I had been looking for a chance to get even ever since.

"Where do you come into all this?" she wanted to know.

"The big tunas can't make a move without their geopolitical-expert consultant," I said.

"So you're employed as a consultant?" I began to be suspicious of this line of questioning. It was what Hamilton Burger would have called badgering the witness.

"I am," I admitted.

Her eyes flashed with satisfaction. "Then trading in Indoil is against SEC regulations," she said primly. "Moreover, it is illegal for your relatives and anyone you may have taken into your confidence. I believe, by the way, there is a prison downstate for white-collar criminals. They say it's practically a country club. It's where they sent Governor Kerner. I'll send cookies."

She made an ostentatious return to the memo she was typing. I was beginning to see how hard it was going to be to stay one up on Laura Westin.

"Sorry," I mumbled. "Just trying to be helpful."

Her face brightened slightly. "There must be some way to make use of this information," I encouraged her. "I mean, it's like being one of the chosen who have early notice of the outcome at Waterloo."

She stopped typing and a ruminative look passed across her face. Suddenly her expression brightened most perceptibly.

"Why, I do believe it might work," she said. "I can't think of a single regulation it would violate. Yes, I believe it would be perfectly legal."

"What's that?"

"Selling Tidelands short."

Sorel met me in the little cubicle from which he oversees his traders on the floor of the Merc. "Look at that SOB," he said. "Just missed a trade. He doesn't have the temperament."

The man Sorel was pointing to was jumping up and down and gesticulating with both hands. It wasn't his fault that he was five feet six and the man who got the trade was six feet five and two forty.

"I'm afraid I'm gonna have to fire him," Sorel said sadly. "You either have the temperament or you don't. Did you ever think of trying floor trading?"

"Not recently," I conceded. I'm about five eleven and one sixty and my voice squeaks when I attempt to shout.

"Probably just as well," Sorel said, sizing me up. "You're not a bad racquet man, but I'm not sure you have the temperament. Now that runner, I think he may have it."

Sorel pointed to a kid who looked like he might be trying to catch on as a free agent with the Bears. Sorel had the temperament himself. He was supposed to have been a pretty good linebacker prospect at Northwestern until he tore up his knee. He did have a slight limp, but it disappeared the moment he walked onto a racquetball court. For a big guy he had some tricky moves.

"About the Indoil angle," I said.

"It's a neat one, all right," Sorel agreed. "Hey, lookit, that goddamn hunk of beef just blew the signal."

"Say, does anybody ever hit anybody out there?" I wondered.

"Do they ever," Sorel said. "It's a five-hundred-buck fine, too. I once saw a hot rookie take out a senior trader with one punch and flip five singles on his chest. Money well spent."

"Like Indoil?" I said. I value the opinion of people who call hundreds singles.

Sorel confirmed Crockett's story. Indoil had gone on a binge buying Indonesian tracts and was now in danger of Chapter 11. It was bad news for the fellows in Jakarta who were used to taking 10 percent off the top.

"They'll do the deal with Crockett?"

"You bet your ass. They'd do a deal with Moshe Dayan before giving up the bribe and the skim. Hey, I told that SOB to get rid of his inventory of pounds." I was trying to work out what the British pound had to do with the Indoil deal when I heard Sorel's clerk relay the message to the floor.

"Can you see any peculiar angles to the deal?"

"Just one," Sorel said. "What does he want with an ivory-tower nincompoop like you for a negotiator?"

"Why *does* he need me?" I asked.

"Oh, it must be his backers," Sorel said. "If he's right, everybody cleans up. If the deal blows up, he can always say a certificated card-carrying ivory-tower asshole signed off on it. There's probably no precedent in Texas tort law for shareholder-liability suits against tenured university professors."

"That's comforting," I said.

"There is one other little oddity," Sorel said. "Your chum Crockett must be president of the Chamber of Commerce down there. I ran across his name the other day on a Ten-K."

"Ten-K?"

"Annual report, to you mystics."

"Oh," I said.

"Little electronics company called Tech Systems. It just struck me at the time. An oil man, and there he was on the Board of Directors. He didn't seem the type."

"What type is that?"

"Well, he's bondable, OK," Sorel said. "I just didn't see him as a Utility Infielder."

"Oh, he isn't, he isn't," I assured Sorel. "He's strictly a Home Run Hitter, and you can take my word for it."

"Well, there's some explanation," Sorel said. "Maybe he's a brigadier in the Air Force Reserve. Or a deacon in a small, select denomination. Or a Mason, maybe. Hell, he probably went to one of the Academies."

"He went to Princeton," I said.

"And with that shit-eater accent. There you are: The CEO at Tech Systems was probably his college roommate." But Sorel didn't seem to be convincing himself. "Or here's an idea. I bet they make high-tech drill bits. Or drilling wire, or, let's see, seismic-testing shit like Litton. Everybody got into that shit in the seventies. You'll probably find a small wholly owned subsid in the annual report."

"Do you still have it?"

"Sorry, I'm afraid I tossed it. The less you know about what a company does the better you trade."

"Business is just business," I said profoundly.

"And Saturday night is sex," Sorel said. "Just don't run it by a connoisseur. There is always a reason for everything, it's just that you don't find it out until it's too late to do you any good. It's a Dallas company. The CEO is probably Crockett's brother-in-law. Means a quick ten thou director's fee, two meetings a year, probably a swift kickback to the bro. The rich never miss an easy ten thou. Only ordinary slobs worry about propriety."

"Like you and me," I said.

"Speak for yourself, white man," Sorel said. He was leading me by the arm into an empty cubicle. "By the way, your old pals from Murder Incorporated caught up with me while you were in Dallas. Caught me as I was leaving the trading floor. Wanted to know about your backhand. I thought you should know."

"There's a theory that I'm up for Undersecretary of State Far East," I said. For a moment I really tried to think what I might have done to make an impression on George Shultz. I couldn't. I just couldn't. "What kind of stuff did they ask?"

"Wanted to know if you played racquetball drunk or on drugs or with unusual political opinions. I told them that you rolled out at six steady as a rock but practiced deception with a wicked reverse corner. I said I could personally endorse you for Postmaster General."

It was old news, and Sorel says you shouldn't let old news bother you. The market never discounts the same news twice. What bothered me a little, though, was the new bit of info on Crockett. Let the Marxists rant and rave, I just wasn't ready to believe that the Interlocking Directorate extended to putting oil wildcatters on the boards of little electronics companies. I didn't approve of it either. I just didn't see what an oil man would have to contribute.

5.
TSY

Genius, Grampa Jack used to say, is not knowing every damn thing, it is knowing how to find a thing when you need to know it. Another of Grampa Jack's sayings was, Be who or whatever you are. I have a feeling it was directed at Gran and referred primarily to an individual's inalienable right to scratch where he itched, but I have occasionally attached a more philosophical meaning to it. I am a man whose first instinct in a crisis is to look something up in a book.

The only one handy on the spur of the moment was Standard & Poor's *Stock Guide,* which was sent out by my broker in appreciation for the two or three thou he had clipped me for in the last year. Tech Systems occupied line 43 on pages 214 and 215, to wit:

43 TSY Tech Systems NY, T A — 179 14975 Elec sys&eq def 47 ½ 27 5/8 21¼ 29 22 3/8 9916 28½

27 28 14 43 1970 Q.12½ 3−15−85 2−15 .12½
.50 .44 48.3 277. 167. 12−31−84 155 21337
Del.05 1.28 1.57 1.89 E2.35 1.95 3 mo Ma .41

As best I could decipher, it meant some or all of the following: Tech Systems was traded over the New York and Toronto Exchanges with ticker symbol TSY. It was rated A− for financial strength, had $1 par value, was owned by 179 institutions that held a total of almost 15 million shares, and had ranged in price between $47 and $.50 per share over the past twelve years, and somewhat more narrowly in recent years, closing at 28. It had a PE of 14. It had paid dividends since 1970 at a current quarterly rate of $.12½, had current assets almost double current liabilities, long-term debt of $155 million, and just over 21 million shares outstanding. I began to see what Sorel meant about the value of fundamental information. I was sure it all meant something to somebody.

Sorel's secretary sent over a pair of charts* that looked like this:

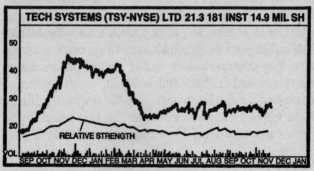

*See Appendix E, p. 275.

```
50│        x   x
  │        x o o x
  │        x   o o x
40│    x   x   o o
  │    x o x   o
  │    x o x   o
  │ x  x       o                   x
30│ x o x         o x x x   x   x o
  │x x o        o o o o x x x o x x o x x x  x  x x
  │x o          o o o   o o   o o x o o x o o
  │x                              o o
20│
```

On the back of one of them, there was a note:

Mr. Sorel says not to worry, TSY just got hit with the other high techs in the summer of 1983. He says it's in a long-term accumulation pattern.

It was Laura Westin who suggested *Market Values*. She even knew where it was in the library. She read it every Friday when it came in. She would have been more than happy to get it for me, but she felt I needed the experience. TSY was alphabetical under "Aerospace/Defense," and the man at the reference desk watched me like a hawk lest I cop the whole section for private use. The long-term chart was more promising than the one Sorel had, which perhaps contained a lesson about life.

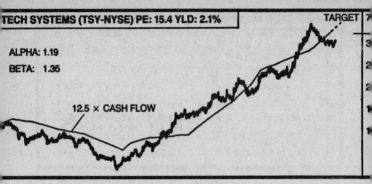

ALPHA: 1.19
BETA: 1.35

12.5 × CASH FLOW

The page contained about ten times as many numbers as the S&P *Guide*. It was nice to know that they were there, so I could refer to them if ever I needed them. Sorel had already warned me off the narrative. "Useless to traders. If true, it's already in the stock. If false, it's the hook that catches the suckers." I went ahead and read it anyway, even though I knew he was right.

Although Tech Systems has been in investor disfavor now for over a year, we have not changed our long-term opinion. Earnings continue to come in on target, and we are confident of our $2.30 estimate.

We project further yearly gains in the 20–25% range. The cost-effectiveness of TSY's major product line was demonstrated when Israel used its American-made ECM equipment to devastate Syrian air and ground forces in the summer of 1982. Tech Systems is positioned in markets with the highest rates of growth and receives a good share of retrofitting business as refinements to existing weapons come on stream.

Headlines about defense budget cuts are not a serious concern. Despite analysts' skittishness about a company that derives so much of its revenue from secret or "black" programs, the backlog continues to grow at its historic 20% annual rate. A small diamond at TSY is its role in the rebuilding of America's intelligence capability. Because of the stringent qualification requirements and constraints on open bidding, the profit margins are large. It is estimated that TSY's sales as primary contractor plus global follow-on sales could reach $1 billion over the next five years. It is our opinion that the current weakness in the shares has been overdone. The shares are timely, and 3–5 year potential is large.

6.
Ghost

I asked Westin to send off for the most recent Tech
Systems Annual Report. I was going to have to send
her flowers or take her to lunch or throw something
extra into the Christmas pool. In the meantime I
took time to ask politely. If there is one thing that
pays off in life, it is being polite to secretaries. I even
took the trouble to ask about her cats.

"I don't have any cats," she said. "I just like
pictures of cats."

I praised the quality of the photographs. She
wanted to know if Mr. Sorel thought Tech Systems
was a hot stock, and I told her we weren't sure yet.
She wrote it down in her academic planner just the
same.

It was Tidelands that our consortium eventually

conducted its raid in. Sorel shorted* five thousand at 31. I also suspected him of buying Indoil calls,† probably through an out of town broker. I didn't want to know.

I shorted eight hundred Tidelands myself against my broker's firm advice. He thought the oils were beginning to firm. Just trust me on this one, I told him.

Westin shorted four hundred in her trading account.

I got the Indonesia tour d'horizon out to Crockett by express mail two days before Christmas. Helen and Jeremy called on Christmas Day, and Lieberman came on to say hello just to show there were no hard feelings.

Crockett met with his executive committee on December 27 and had a private meeting with his bankers and investment partners the following morning. On January 2 I received an Express Mail parcel of cigars that looked like armor-piercing ordnance. I also received a plane ticket, a contract, and negotiating parameters on both price structure and lifting schedule. The plane ticket was first class all the way. I told Laura Westin it was all the sushi you could eat on the leg out of Tokyo. I had once been in the very first row of second-class seats where you can watch. She just sniffed.

On January 4 the visa arrived from the Indonesian Consulate in New York. It is faster than the embassy, and tends to ask fewer questions. On the

*Short: to sell shares not owned in the hope of buying them back at a lower price
†See Appendix F, p. 276.

first trading day of the year, Tidelands obliged us all by dropping a full point.

That afternoon I confirmed my travel plans with the dean. He had no objections. Academics only pretend to a disdain of the material world. No group is better informed about retirement benefits or mortgage rates. I could see the notion of an endowed chair in Southeast Asian studies beginning to take shape in the dean's head.

I called in my three graduate students in Malay *pantuns* and gave them a translation so impossible that they would not even inquire about my whereabouts for a couple of weeks. By all standards I should have felt good about the world. I had been playing racquetball every day over the break and working in the library on the Tokyo Agreements. I was plenty tired. The trouble was, I wasn't sleepy. I had about tricked myself, though, with a tall Scotch, three aspirin, and an early Len Deighton. The truth was, it was that highly critical panic period when you know you have to conk out in five minutes, ten at the outside, or else.

That's why it was so irritating when the phone rang at ten minutes to midnight. It was even more irritating when it turned out to be Big Gus Friedler calling from Ithaca. He was drunk as a hoot owl, or maybe a scrooch owl, and he was calling from a pay phone at some kind of low dive for Cornell cowboys. He was also trying to whisper. Have you ever heard a drunk try to whisper over the sound of Willie Nelson?

"Gotta apologize, Keith, gotta apologize," he blubber-whispered.

"That's quite all right," I said. I meant for it to come out icy and distant and stiffly correct, but it came out the way you talk to a friend you haven't heard from in a while. That's the way it is when you are caught off guard.

"What you gotta understand is the pressure," he said. "Shit, they do half the funding for the major journals. They keep half the programs above water. I gotta wife. I got three kids. I gotta publish, man. I gotta get grants."

"What the hell are you talking about?" My tone of voice was getting more like it. "I've got a wife and a kid myself."

"Just take it easy, man. What I'm saying is, you gotta understand the pressure." Then he added, "I'm trying to warn you."

It was then that I realized Big Gus wasn't just drunk. I had seen him pick up skin diving in a morning, and I had seen him tell the editor of a top journal to kiss the place they hide the moon, but right now he was scared.

"Who is they?"

"Like the Taipei Ghost" was all he said.

"Listen, Gus," I said, but there was nothing on the other end anymore but Willie doing "You Were Always on My Mind." The Taipei Ghost was what we called an inexplicable American who had turned up with full credentials at the Taiwan Symposium in '77. We had decided he was some kind of spook. Now I really wasn't sleepy.

7.

Jeremy Bentham

I called Jeremy when I landed in San Francisco. It occurred to me to drop in on the Liebermans, but I thought better of it. As long as Lieberman had taken a job at San Francisco State just to get away from me, I thought I should honor his good intentions. To tell the truth, I wasn't up for another bout of Lieberman being decent about things. I was the one who held the option of being decent. I had tried to tell myself that when your wife left you, it didn't much matter who she left you for. It mattered all right. I wasn't at all pleased with the idea of Jeremy growing up under the influence of a high-IQ dufus whose lifework consisted of exploring whether Graham Greene got his Catholicism and his Marxism properly mixed. Jeremy would grow to manhood without eating a grape or a head of lettuce. I know professors all too well, and I also know the tricks they have for influencing impressionable youth.

Jeremy sounded good enough. He gave a very satisfying account of an afternoon of chamber music His Scholarship had taken him to. The set of people who dislike chamber music is too inclusive to be meaningful, but people who dislike it actively and knowledgeably are a special and secret elite. I could smell the odor of Lieberman's displeasure over the phone.

Helen came on then to notify me that she was worried about Jeremy. He was pale and too thin and was having trouble making friends at his new school. His grades had fallen off (with high school only a year away, when they really start to count), and he had gotten suspended twice for fighting on the schoolgrounds. Worse yet, he seemed to have lost his enthusiasm for the violin.

"Stuff his violin," I said.

"I didn't hear that."

"Break it in pieces. Use it for kindling. Put the slivers under Marty's fingernails."

"Marty thinks he calls you on the sneak," she said.

"Bug the phone," I suggested. "Bug his room, too."

"Last week I found a lingerie ad in his dresser drawer."

"Good," I said. "He's got the right idea."

"Keith, please." Her voice shifted deeper into her official worried tone. "How long do you have before your flight?"

I told her I had about six hours.

"I'd like you to have a talk with him. There's a weapons and armor show at the Art Institute. He wants to go and Marty won't take him. I'll put him in a taxi and you can put him in a taxi home." She really was worried.

On the whole I was unimpressed by the lances. I thought I would try a few alternatives before I attempted to inflict any harm with one. It wasn't until we got to the halberds and pikes that I saw anything I could do damage with.

"You're quite right, Dad," Jeremy informed me. He had grown five inches while losing five pounds, and Helen wasn't kidding about pale. "Swiss pikemen proved capable of breaking up cavalry charges, especially on mountainous terrain. It was the end of medieval warfare. Of course it was artillery that really swung the balance."

I was sure he was reading it, but for the life of me I couldn't find the little card.

"Personal firearms like the blunderbuss and harquebus were far less accurate and effective," he went on. "That accounts for the persistent use of cutting, thrusting, and hacking hand weapons well into the eighteenth century."

"You're reading all this," I said, but Jeremy was off examining a row of pikes from the Thirty Years' War. They all looked the same to me, but he was stopping to note the peculiarities of each one. It was like Eskimos being able to detect seventeen different kinds of snow.

"I didn't realize there was any such actual thing

as a blunderbuss," I said. "I thought it was the German word for asshole. Your mother tells me there is cause for complaint about your grades."

"Um," he grunted. "Tilly's men carried these long blades in the Bavarian campaign. Wallenstein's army used the ones with the fancy handles."

He said it with a *V* sound and an *H* inserted between the *S* and the *T*. I was pretty sure they didn't put the phonetics on the cue cards. "Where do you learn all this shit?"

"Here and there. I look things up. I check out the books mentioned in the bibliographies and footnotes. I went through the library shelves on war and military history—sometimes that makes me break out into a related subject. The words I look up in Marty's French and German dictionaries."

"Marty must love that."

"Marty's a blunderbuss." He looked up to be sure I got it. He had been listening, all right.

"You really ought to pull those grades up."

"How?"

"Answer more questions correctly. The questions they are asking in school. You want to quit violin?" I offered.

"Maybe," he said warily.

"You just retired," I said. "Tell Mom I said so."

He walked ahead through an arched door into a long room with glass cases down the center and around the walls. The cases contained about thirty-seven Medieval Three-Piece Suits. I liked the helmets in the shape of mad dogs and wild pigs. The rest of it provided an additional insight into the demise of *Tyrannosaurus rex*.

"Before you got into one of these you made sure you went to the bathroom," I said.

"Some of them were equipped," Jeremy said. Then blurted, "Do you think you could whip Marty in a fair fight?"

"With what? With witty one-liners at twenty paces?"

"With blunderbusses." The idea of a fight with Marty Lieberman was moderately hilarious. Even Jeremy could see that.

"What about Mitch Metzger?" Metzger had been the Little League coach who had to take Jeremy. He had been in the Astro organization, but his real calling was winning Little League championships. He had thrown Jeremy in for the last half inning to comply with regulations. At the end of every practice he stuck his outfielders fifty yards behind the fence and had his pitcher serve up cripples while he cracked homers like the Little League Babe Ruth. "Could you whip Mitch Metzger in a fair fight, Dad?"

"I don't see the point," I said. "I don't see that Mitch has laid waste my vineyards or besieged my cities."

"But could you?"

"You think Tilly and Wallenstein went around looking for fair fights?" I said. "Avoid fights. Run. Hide. But if you get into a fight, do everything in your power to make it unfair."

"Whatever," Jeremy said sullenly. He had started to lag back while I looked at swords that were gradually slimming down to rapiers and épées. His expression made it clear what I had become: a Knight of the Medieval Order of Men Who Run and Hide _ from Fair Fights.

"Been in any fights yourself lately?"

"A couple," he said. "Whose idea was it to name me Jeremy anyway?"

"Your mother's," I said. "She insisted. It was my idea to make it Jeremy Bentham."

"Who was Jeremy Bentham?"

"He was a philosopher who believed that people should be reasonable," I said. "When he died he left his money to the College of London on the condition that they stuff his body and keep it in a glass case. And they have to bring it out for meetings of the board of overseers."

"And did they?"

"For a hundred and fifty years. You can go visit him the next time you're in London."

"He was kind of tough," Jeremy proposed.

"He was tough-minded," I said.

Jeremy took it all in, but I could tell he wasn't quite convinced.

"I miss you, Dad," he said.

"I miss you, too," I said. "If you have any more problems at school, you give me a call."

I hailed a taxi at the entrance and managed to restrain myself from instructing him on how to tip. As the taxi pulled away I added Jeremy to my short list of little nagging worries. My briefcase was full of them. One was the article on the Tokyo Agreements. I had run across a complicating factor in a long footnote. It seemed from certain records of the oil ministry that Suharto's choice of Tokyo, far from being coincidental, had been intended to convey some sort of message.

Another little nag was the last conversation I had had with the dean. He hadn't been quite sure whether he should share my personnel file with the two men who had come around, but in the end he had decided that it was pretty harmless. I could tell that he was dying to know what kind of job I was going to be offered in Washington, not just for gossip value but because he was already adding up how many low-paid lecturers he could buy with my salary line.

Then there was the annual report for Tech Systems. Westin had placed it in my hands as I was leaving for the airport. The cover had a cute little logo. It seemed like a good little growth company with low debt, a small headquarters staff, and lots of smart engineers with security clearances who had advanced degrees from MIT and Rice. They made gizmos that would do things like tell you what your electric typewriter was typing at a range of four hundred yards through two feet of concrete. I wondered what they made that they weren't willing to talk about? One thing they didn't make was drill bits or drilling wire or any kind of sophisticated electronic equipment for seismic tests whatsoever. I had gone over it with a fine-tooth comb on the leg out from San Francisco, and if they had anything to do with oil it was strictly TS Crypto. Crockett was right up there on the Board of Directors, though, along with six corporate officers, a former ambassador, a retired admiral, a black woman twobird, and my old acquaintance Oren Lewes.

8.
Gara-Gara

The 747 struggled into the air and bade farewell to the Western Hemisphere with a great roar. I glanced at the Golden Gate, which was so much itself that it was hard to believe the builders hadn't had the aerial view in mind. As soon as we achieved low orbit I got up and began an inspection of my fellow passengers. Flights out of major cities are like that trick about two people at large dinner parties having the same birthday. The median number of faces that are vaguely familiar is about 2.5. It's purely statistical. That's why I made up my mind not to worry too much about the tall man sitting three rows behind me.

About forty minutes out the stewardess came around and took down a list of my personal preferences. I looked her up and down with modest display of appetite—a true Singapore Girl, tall, willowy, Chinese, perfect, and completely enclosed in a *nolo me tangere* aura as visible as a glass case. "You will be wanting a sleeping berth?"

I could think of a use for one, but I didn't trust myself if I got started again on preferences.

"There are pillows if you change your mind," she said.

I was trying to decide whether to comply with the optional suggestion of keeping seat belts fastened "for comfort" when my seatmate introduced herself. "We're overflow."

"She means we were overbooked on JAL." Her husband reached across to offer his hand. "The rest of our group will be four hours behind us."

"The last shall be first," his wife said brightly. "It's the Toyota Superdealers annual tour. Jess here sold more Toyotas than any dealer in Alabama, Louisiana, Mississippi, and Eastern Arkansas."

"It's a formula, actually," Jess confided. "You know that, Hon. It has a factor for options. There's nothing much to selling cars. With the quotas, it's the option loadup they care about. They work it out in Tokyo."

"We're going to Tokyo and Osaka," Hon said. "We're going on a tour of the Toyota plant."

"Sounds like fun," I said. After a discreet interval I buzzed Singapore Girl and accepted that pillow. I had a single strong Scotch chased by three glasses of water, climbed the spiral staircase into the hump, and strapped myself into one of the empty slabs. There were things far worse than sudden death.

I slept until Tokyo, where they trotted us out for exercise in the sunless corridors of Narita. I made sure Familiar Face was ahead of me in line and watched until he split off into the group going to Customs and Immigration. At the same moment I remembered who he was. I had seen his picture in the *Times* when he was appointed to the Federal Reserve Board of Governors. I wandered around Narita Holding inspecting the little layered slabs where you can sleep like the dead for four to six hours at a cost of only a few thousand yen. I wasn't ready yet for a trial run at modern mortuary. Instead I walked by the snack bar—it would be interesting to see how rice was evolving as a fast food—but it just didn't meet my conception of breakfast. Anyway, I was saving myself for the sushi.

When we replaned, the Toyota couple was replaced by a brace of Japanese businessmen with briefcase, camera, and calculator. I listened as they speculated in Japanese as to whether I was a tourist or an engineer. Not a tourist, one of them said, not without a wife and not into Jakarta, and not even an American engineer would wear a shabby jacket like that. It really bothered them. I doodled out mock equations on my napkin. An anthropologist, the other one said, the kind who digs, and I smiled and made little scooping motions with my swizzle stick. They fell into a hushed conversation about the pricing opportunities occasioned by the fall in lumber prices.

On every flight to Southeast Asia there is a moment when your life flashes before your eyes. It has about sixteen hours to flash with. It's a little like *gara-gara*, the storm that always takes place in the second act of the shadow plays. It's another lair-batin thing. The ocean boils and bubbles. The bubbling ocean represents the hero's unquiet heart.

We were somewhere over the Ryukyus when Singapore Girl's identical twin and replacement came over the intercom to warn us that there was turbulence over the South China Sea. It was turbulent all right. I watched her strap the serving cart down and buckle herself in. Mainly I was concerned about the sushi. The really good stuff has a half-life of about ninety seconds, and we were already well over an hour away from Tokyo food service. I was also wondering if they would keep serving sushi during the movie. It was definitely a bad sign when the storm began to take my mind off the sushi. I checked my seat belt again and told myself that I had led a reasonably good life. I had slept with at least four truly world-class women, I liked hot food and had a stomach that could take it, and I had once watched a man being tortured. I have never been tortured myself. The trouble with my life was that there were always things going on around me that I didn't understand at the time. I was terrific at languages and word problems, though.

As far as I know, I was the only person who ever maxed the ALAT. ALAT stands for Army Language Aptitude Test. It was made up of little paragraphs followed by questions, like a language textbook. One of the paragraphs was about *lingans* and *dorgans,* students and teachers. It had Malay nondeclension, Latinate conjugation, and German sentence structure. Dorgan lingan dorgat. Teacher teaches student. Lingan ALAT lingat. Student learns ALAT. It was a cinch.

They sent me to Monterey to learn Vietnamese and to Fort Holabird to learn to pick locks and then to Chuong Thien Province, which was where I watched Captain Han use torture in interrogations. Which was also where I met Xuan. I would probably have married her except for the child she said was her nephew. Instead I went home and married Helen Lett.

It was the same basic aptitude that enabled me to learn Bahasa in three months (a variant of Malay, written originally in Arabic, then Dutch, then English script and phonetics, with certain idiosyncratic inflections) and pick up enough old Javanese (a socially stratified language, you don't want to know how it works) to be accused by the orals committee of being from a missionary family. Also a smattering of Mandarin, Russian, and Urdu. Also some Japanese. I could probably have learned Esperanto if I had been that particular kind of idiot. And all I ever wanted in life was to be a big-league ball player.

I still can't quite piece together how Helen got involved with Lieberman.

I could tell that Singapore Girl II wasn't caring much for the turbulence. Stewardesses are flying weather vanes. When they don't mind it, I don't mind it. When they get nervous, I get nervous. Singapore II was nervous. I could tell that all the sushi you can eat was going to turn out to be one of those daydreams. I would be lucky to get a couple of pieces.

I started reassuring myself with all the things you tell yourself under the circumstances. Number One, no 747 has ever gone down as a result of bad weather. Number Two, a 747 is safer than riding across town on a CTA bus. Number Three, if it wasn't safe, people wouldn't fly on them (although you may say this gives the public too much credit). Number Four, the pilots are superbly trained, broadly experienced, and hardly ever high on anything to sustain their flagging biorhythms, etch etch. After Number Two they start to get a little tenuous.

There is a passage where James Bond runs into some bumpy flying on his way to an adventure in Istanbul. He is on his way to steal a decoder and seduce a beautiful Russian agent, but the thing that interests me is the way Bond handles the storm. He simply withdraws. He goes into a private storm room. He puts down the Eric Ambler thriller he is reading and goes into a trance. It's an almost perfect description of samadhi, the Indonesian form of meditation by which the hero in the shadow play calms the storm.

I must have worried the storm into submission. Singapore II had to wake me for the descent. When I pushed up the shade I could already see orange tile roofs and paddies like lakes of glass. The pile of sushi in the galley was covered with little slime rainbows, and I had only gotten four pieces. The Japanese businessmen were busy filling out entry forms, which did not, however, prohibit them from extracting Indonesian timber and copper, working them around a bit, and selling them back to the Indonesians at a 500 percent markup. One of them got out his calculator, while his bombardier checked to see if his Nikon was fully loaded. He gestured toward the window, and sure enough, it was target registration photos he wanted.

"They call Jakarta the urban village," I said in

Japanese. "In Singapore they use the Malay word for 'village.' *Kampong*. It is not altogether flattering."

I left him to ponder the fact that I was speaking in Japanese. As if on cue, the pilot banked again to provide a view of the Artholoka building poking its head up from thatched huts and footpaths and tropical canopy. With more than one thousand people to the square mile, we were looking down at the most densely populated piece of real estate on earth, notwithstanding the occasional demurral from Bangladesh. I could begin to see them, walking up and down market roads and lumbering behind oxen in paddy ditches, doing all the random things people do when you see them in large numbers from a good distance. If you liked that sort of thing, it was a real tourist kick, number one in its category. The Grand Canyon and World Trade Towers of teeming masses. The Japanese was smiling and pointing and pretending as hard as he could that I hadn't really spoken in Japanese. We were both breathing a sigh of relief. There was still some Third World out there, no farther away than your nearest travel agent.

9.
Halim

Halim started out as a military base, but in recent years it has replaced Kemajoran as Jakarta's international airport. It is one of the more sprawling of the world's major airports, with sections of military housing still intact. There is only a modest monument to mark the spot where they murdered the generals.

There is an element of parody in every Third World air terminal. They have the booths with glass windows, all right, and the little stacks of thin document paper in nonstandard sizes with delicate, almost ethereal writing, and the bored men in unstarched uniforms who seem determined not to break out in sweat. The men look like they don't know quite what to do except try to look refined, and the booths are a little like gag doors set up in the middle of a stage. You can't help wondering if there is really a fence somewhere, or if you could just leave the queue and walk out into the country.

A middle-aged couple was staging a little skit directly ahead of me in line. They were mainly complaining about the baggage handlers, but you could tell they weren't insane about the passport control and customs people either.

Danauer had provided my civilian training in that kind of thing. Neither a complainer nor a criticizer of complainers be, was his opinion. He had a sort of storm-room theory of his own about bureaucrats and baggage handlers, and as far as he was concerned it was more important than the storm room you use on bumpy plane rides. "Just remember that when that man's father was picking up a missionary, the missionary told him to put seven sticks in the ground, take one out each day at sunup, and meet the boat the day there were none left." I could never quite work out who were the butts of Danauer's little anecdotes.

The couple was busy ugly Americaning their way inch by inch through the passport queue. He manufactured machine tools in Cleveland that the Japs hadn't managed to make a decent copy of, and she normally had unusually liberal views for a Republican canvasser. I knew them a good deal better than this by the time we were in sight of the window. I seemed to be their primary audience. At any rate they did most of their talking backward in my direction.

The line *was* moving unusually slowly. I dropped

my passport on the counter and let my eyes drift toward the declarations desk. A voice said, "McCallum Keith."

"Yes."

I picked up right away on the absence of the honorific. The Javanese are like Germans about honorifics. The omission usually means something.

"You will come with me."

I did not miss the declarative syntax. The Javanese are very polite people. I also noticed the omission of the please.

They brought me to a room no larger than a large closet or cupboard, and without windows. It had a low ceiling, a single light bulb, an empty table, and a single chair. The official gestured for me to sit and then departed without giving any indication as to when he would be back. I recognized the procedure from my army days. I didn't have NEED-TO-KNOW.

The single drawer in the table contained eighteen paper clips, three cigarette butts, a single vacant sheet of that ethereal paper (made of the finest Oriental fabric but folded carelessly and coated with dust), and two Styrofoam cups with decaying residue of the original coffee that Mohammad II's traders introduced to the islands. After what seemed like an hour but must really have been twenty minutes at the nervous-boredom discount, a different official poked his head around the door. He had stripes on his uniform that I had not noticed on the first official. He had three of them in fact. He was either a sergeant, a captain, a colonel, or a lieutenant general.

I was guessing captain. I asked him what was going on.

"You sit here," he cut me off. His voice walked a thin line between peremptory command and practical suggestion. It might have held a hint of promise. It held more than a hint of rudeness. It was excellent psychological warfare.

I told myself that they couldn't very well beat, torture, or kill me. Alan Pope had bombed a church in Sumatra, *while a service was going on,* and they hadn't done any of the above to him. If he had happened to like rice and hot peppers, he would have been none the worse for wear five years later when Bobby Kennedy sprung him. I hadn't done anything remotely as bad as bombing a church. What had I done, anyway?

Another twenty-minute hour passed, and I was just about to get up and try the door when Three Stripes reappeared. "You come with me."

He took me down a couple of corridors and through a large office to a glassed-in corner cubicle. I guessed that it was the room where drug and customs interrogations took place. I wondered if Republican Machine Tools of Cleveland had stashed his cocaine in one of my pockets. My suitcase and carry-on bag were stacked against the wall. Behind the desk was a pudgy official whose epaulets showed that he had made it to the fourth rung. My passport was open on his desk.

"You are McCallum Keith Alistair."

It just had to be a question. It had all the characteristics of a question except word order and voice inflection. I decided to treat it as a question. I also decided that he could work out the order of my name, if pressed. I nodded.

"You are university teacher."

If it was *This Is Your Life,* it had a weak opening. I nodded, though.

"You are in Indonesia for purpose of business."

He scored one more time.

"What business is this?"

He was a man who recognized a real question when it came out of his mouth. I told him that I was not at liberty to say. I was sorry, but it was of a confidential nature. Now if he would just make a telephone call for me . . .

Four Stripes growled. "Papers not in order," he grunted.

I confess that I was a bit snappish. Whatever this was going to be, I thought indignation was a pretty good opening response.

"You will see you cannot enter this country without proper documents." I noticed that he was holding my passport open to the visa page. We went through the question about my business a couple more times. It was like a runaway computer loop.

"Date on visa is incorrect," he said finally. Was it possible? I had looked over the visa when it arrived from New York. He finally broke down and let me look at it. The Konsulat Jenbrae Republik Indonesia in New York stated that I was permitted into Java and/or Bali for single/several journeys for a period of thirty days within the three-month period beginning January 10.

There was just one problem. It was beginning January 10 of last year. It was the kind of simpleminded mistake I make in my checkbook until about the fifteenth of February. It had arrived on January

4, which meant some absentminded clerk had stamped it on the first workday of January without changing the date. I was wondering if Four Stripes would believe that, or if some sense of Third World protocol would make him feel compelled to put me on the next plane out, but he was looking at a spot outside the cubicle. I tracked his stare to a spot across the room where another official was busy apologizing to a young woman. He had some spectacular hand gestures, but it was hard to look at anything but the woman.

She had the kind of beauty that makes the fillings in your teeth hurt. Also she looked familiar. Then I had it. It was Xuan. Well, it was almost Xuan. And she hadn't aged a minute in twenty years. Of course, she was not wearing a cheongsam. Her dress was now fully Western and chic, probably Paris or Milan.

The official was closing in on our cubicle with Almost Xuan in close pursuit. When he got to the door of the cubicle, I noticed almost simultaneously the five stripes on his epaulets and the way Four Stripes got to his feet. Indonesians have a strong sense of hierarchy, and so do I.

"You are Professor Doctor McCallum please." Five Stripes ignored the subordinate. It was an unfortunate misunderstanding. He hoped I had not been inconvenienced. I was, naturally, quite free to go. I had a truly warm feeling until I remembered that it used to be Doctor Engineer Sukarno Please too.

It was all just an unfortunate mishap, of course, but it would also have been a nifty way to remind an unpopular guest that he had crossed over into a tightly controlled little island. Could they really have worked that sort of thing out with the New York Consulate? "I am Siti," the woman was saying. "Moko is my uncle." I kept trying to think about the visa mistake, but I can't think straight when I am looking straight at a woman that beautiful and she is looking straight at me. They definitely knew how to keep a fellow off balance.

10.
Slametan

Siti spent the first half of the drive into Jakarta apologizing and the second half explaining. Her countrymen (she explained) were backward over-organized louts. The passport office was staffed by family idiots. Jakarta traffic was a reflection of the national insanity (this while casually weaving among four ill-defined lanes).

Moko was her uncle and Moko was also her boss. She was just back from Switzerland. She missed it terribly. It had been decided that she would go to work for the oil ministry. Meeting me at the airport had been her first real job, and now she had bungled it. She would have been on time if a bemo* driver had not hit a drug-crazed cyclist and thrown her off

---

*Acronym for *becak motor*, or official van. They are notorious for tooling around Jakarta at high speed with low regard for obstacles in their path.

schedule. It was as if the cyclist had given his life to ruin her whole morning.

While she talked I picked out the National Sports Stadium, which the Russians had built and which reminded me of the Harry S Truman Sports Complex in Kansas City. Then there was the Freedom Statue with Eternal Flame, referred to by the locals as Waiter Bringing Ice Cream. The stretch on Jalan Thamrin with the billboard of tan revolutionaries with rifles and bandoliers facing down a pygmy Uncle Sam now held the world's largest Coca-Cola ad. Look it up in Guinness. I had never seen anything quite like the way she drove. Her story was getting more and more credible. We made the half-turn where skyscrapers begin to grow up out of the thatched huts and pulled up in front of the Jakarta Mandarin. I wondered if she had driven that way in Switzerland.

"I am to see that you are comfortably established," she said. "My uncle requests the honor of your presence for a *slametan*."

I asked the occasion.

"My safe return from Europe has been mentioned," she said. "I believe that in reality it is to celebrate my uncle's reluctant acceptance of greater responsibilities."

God, but did she speak English with straight white teeth.

On the road to Bogor I listened as she regaled me with tales of the charm and physical beauty of Switzerland. I thought about my last meeting with Moko, when I had been in the way of doing him a large favor. I had modestly neglected to mention it to Crockett. Moko was one of the young bureaucrats who had been swept into power by the overthrow of Sukarno. After the murder of the generals, young people had taken to the streets, led by KAMI and KAPPI.* They had chanted things like Cut the Inflation Rate or Improve the Current Accounts Balance. As I've said, it was an unusual revolution.

Moko was one of the leaders of KAPPI. I met him a decade later. Danauer had given me a letter of introduction and insisted that I seek him out at the first Kuala Lumpur Conference. The Pertamina† scandal had just broken, and I was able to point out to Moko that the American banks had an interest in keeping their Indonesian loans on the books. I even suggested some ways of restructuring to get the paper past the auditors. Moko got a promotion out of it, the banks got to pay their dividends, the Indos met their restructured payments, and I got the satisfaction of having contributed to a constructive outcome. Cast your bread upon the waters, the book says.

Moko met us at the door. His handshake was all nostalgia for K.L. and his greeting to Siti had just the right note of avuncular disapproval. He had come up in the world, all right. His summer bungalow would have cost a good four hundred thou in, say, Marin County, and you might think half of that in the hills of Bogor, but twice was more like it. I counted six Mercedeses and three Bayerischers in the drive.

*The high school and university student associations
†The Indonesian national oil company. Revelations of massive graft and embezzlement put it into technical insolvency in 1975.

In the backyard twenty or thirty guests were already milling around a huge rijsttafel. It was laid out on a long table with the traditional rice volcano in the center. In a genuine slametan the male and female guests would have been talking separately, but this was sort of a slametan in quotation marks. At the real kind, the food is laid out for the spirits to eat, and then, because it is safe to assume after a time that the spirits have had their fill, the guests are allowed to dig in. I could sense that the spirits were going to have to be quick about it.

Moko introduced me to a circle of guests who seemed to be drawn from the upper levels of business and government. Several of them seemed to know something of my work, and they were willing to talk of their own with the occasional guilty glances that take place among the upper classes in a not-quite-open society. There was a lot of talk about "Indonesia" and "development."

"You must understand that we are still an insular people," Moko apologized. "We are intensely interested in ourselves. Everyone present had relatives involved in 1965. Before, we were all Sukarnists. Now we are all Suhartists."

"Piffle and drivel," said a small woman at my elbow. "Listen to Moko play the Indonesian Big Man. Because I am a Sumatran, I will tell you the truth whether it pleases you or not.* Moko was never a Sukarnist. You had to be old enough to remember the Dutch, to be a Sukarnist."

"Certainly Sukarno was a great world figure,"

*Sumatrans are considered by other Indonesians to be unusually contentious.

I said neutrally. He had also been a world-class swordsman, even after he got bald. That was why everybody in the country had to wear those silly hats.

"I danced with Sukarno once," she said. She paused as if savoring the memory. "He talked to me just as we are talking now. He knew something about every subject—art, literature—and he talked just like an ordinary person, not a president in a palace. He was also a wonderful dancer."

I felt a light pressure at my elbow. Siti had decided that I was in need of rescue. "Dalippah can be tiresome," she said. "A typical Sumatran. Always determined to contradict."

"Dalippah?"

"Weren't you introduced? Dalippah is Moko's aunt. My great-aunt. She holds the tourist-bus concession."

Some comic aspect of this concession caused Siti to break into a giggle. At that moment it was decided that the spirits had had all of the food that they were going to get. Moko turned out to be enough of a traditionalist to make the men and women sit separately while they actually ate. Siti greeted this news with a little pout and impudently grabbed a pepper from the base of the volcano. From the very jaws of the spirits, if you will.

It's not that I don't like garden parties. It's just that I'm not *crazy* about them, and from Chicago this one was so ideally located from the standpoint of jet lag. Moko took pity and asked me into his study.

"Let's be American about this," he said. "Please describe for me the proposal of this Mr. Crockett."

I explained Crockett's intentions as clearly as I

could in my present condition. I paraphrased the parts about bankruptcy courts and foreign exchange and omitted the parts about rakeoffs altogether.

"What sort of lifting schedule would Mr. Crockett find satisfactory?"

I didn't have the stamina for a long discussion, so I gave him Crockett's final number.

"I see," he said. He stared into the distance. He didn't attempt to bargain.

"What do you think we should do?" This was an odd sort of negotiation. He made me take his position and I made him take mine. Indonesians are sometimes like that. I told him that Crockett's reasoning was pretty solid. There was also a pretty good chance that oil prices were going to fall. It was a matter of dealing with Crockett now or someone else later.

"Very well, then," he said with finality. "I will present Mr. Crockett's proposition to the committee. A decision of this sort must be made by consensus in our government. In the meantime I suggest that you allow my niece to show you around the island."

I admired Moko's sagacious killing of two birds and also his ability to pick out the precise moment when I was about to topple on my face. He was going to let me go home before the end of the party, but on the way to the door he couldn't resist pointing out items from his collection of arts and crafts. He had some pretty nice ikat and some wedding sarongs carefully separated at the seams for wall hanging. In the foyer there was an oil painting of a young woman who was Almost Siti. It had to be Siti. The style was mannerist, let's say Italian seventeenth century or Russian any period, and it had all the marks of a Sunday painter sweating on the insides of his ears trying to capture a reasonable likeness. I couldn't imagine why on earth Moko let it hang in his foyer.

"Our family heirloom." Moko was reading my mind. I knew it. "I am afraid that in pure aesthetics it does not come up to the weavings. It does have a value beyond its surface merits. The artist, you see, was President Sukarno."

I waited, but he didn't go on to tell me how he had come to own it. I looked now rather more dutifully, taking in the brushstrokes as well as the image. It certainly wasn't good, not by any stretch, but it stood up very well to Eisenhower and Churchill. I looked at it from several angles while my mind performed a couple of rapid calculations. Moko had to get back to his other guests and the actual Siti was already waiting for me in the car. There just wasn't an occasion for asking how Sukarno could have painted a portrait of a woman who would have been no more than seven years old at the time of his death.

11.
Siti

I slept straight through until morning. They had left
the local papers at my door, and there was a bowl of
fruit on the dressing table. I settled back with a
rambutan and some sliced papaya. The headlines
read: IRAN COMPLAINS, PEKING HAILS POL POT, ASSEM-
BLYMAN WARNS AQUINO, WORLD BANK MORALLY OBLIGED.

Siti was waiting in the Mandarin coffee shop.
She seemed to be in a bright enough mood. At least
that was the tone she took as she reviewed the two-
page itinerary she had drawn up on ministry sta-
tionery. We were going to see the flea market on
Jalan Surabaya, Sarinah's (the department store
named after Sukarno's old nurse and, some said, first
mistress), a couple of boutiques (was a theme emerg-
ing?), the wayang museum if I really wanted to, the
old harbor, some shopping spots she knew around
the harbor, the new amusement park called Taman

Mini Indonesia (with a stop for shopping in that neighborhood), and several monuments that were located within convenient walking distance of good specialty shops. If her uncle's consultations dragged on, we could try the shopping in Jogja, or maybe Bandung. Her voiced brightened whenever she had occasion to use the word boutique, but I began to sense a little hesitancy.

"I'm afraid you are going to find this dull."

I shook my head vigorously. I was still doing a palsied no when she completed her thought: "If you do, we could always cut out the monuments."

I assured her that I had already seen the monuments on several occasions, but that it would be my pleasure to take her to dinner. In the meantime there was work which I could accomplish in the National Archives. I was pretty sure I had said the right thing, but her face was starting to cloud.

"My uncle is angry with me," she admitted. I tried to reassure her. I was certain that no man would be very mad with her for very long. I was absolutely sincere. I even gave her a chaste there, there in the neutral territory just above the left shoulder blade, not too firm but not too brotherly either. A beautifully formed tear rolled off the tip of her nose and fell into her coffee with a splash.

I am a good listener. Really I am. The heart of it, of course, was an unhappy love affair. She had been sent off to Switzerland with her father (which meant that Suharto didn't trust him enough for a ministry or distrust him enough to shoot him) and had grown up there. She had run for a couple of years in the adolescent jet set and had had a fling with one Dieter, a German-Swiss twice her age with the Decline of the West winningly etched on his face. When the time came to take up her proper place in Jakarta, she had stalled as long as possible. It made her uncomfortable to think that a thousand peasants had lived their lives at subsistence level so she could go to finishing school in Geneva, but she saw no reason why she should allow this fact to spoil the rest of her life. In the end, though, she had to go home. Even Dieter (by tortuous reasoning which I find it difficult to reconstruct) had agreed that it was for the best.

All I could do for the moment was listen and nod and flick flecks of imaginary dust off my crying shoulder. I was there if needed. I had done worse things with my time. I didn't tell her my true opinion of the German-Swiss or share my instant analysis of Dieter. In the main, I nodded. Things were subtly starting to go my way. I was sleeping, too. While she visited the powder room, I stole a look at the financial page of her *Straits Times*. Indoil had risen another point since the last time I looked. In the last day's trading it was up ⅝ on volume. Tidelands was off a half at 27¾.

Jakarta is not a bad city, really, unless you live in one of the sections where those open concrete aqueducts provide for both drinking water and sewers. It's a little rough, of course. I've heard it said that the muggers in certain areas lack the deep sense of humanism and personal decency one encounters at about seventy-five south in Chicago. Also parts of it lack proper dedication to be picturesque. That was okay by me. Sometimes you're just as happy to be in a place that doesn't dilate your pupils every fifteen minutes. Our first stop was Jalan Surabaya where I bought a large, hairy rakshasa for Westin and a Bima with a huge flesh-tearing fingernail for Jeremy. By a neat bit of broken-field running I managed to catch Siti only three stalls down. I held up the wooden puppets for her to examine. I made Bima say "Hello, pretty girl" by talking out of the side of my mouth, raising and lowering the shaft that supported his head so that he seemed to be breathing.

"How clever you are!" she exclaimed. "For an American."

I made Bima breathe deeper and faster. "It's not difficult for a great dalang,"* I said in my own voice.

"Pfoo," she said. "You don't have wayang† in America."

"But of course we do," I said. "We are developing our own traditions for the shadow plays. Some of the truly great dalangs are now American."

"You're teasing me," she said.

"Not at all. I have personally made the acquaintance of an American master."

"Deep in the American jungle, I suppose," she sniggered.

"Mainly in Washington," I said. Bima still had her fixed with his thyroid eyes, but I had gotten

*Puppet master. A skilled dalang is simultaneously puppeteer, singer, poet, improvisator upon history and current events, scenarist, and impresario; the word is also used as slang for a shifty operator, a puller of strings.
†Indonesian puppet theater is performed with both wooden puppets (wayang golek) and leather shadow puppets. The same plays are sometimes performed by actors wearing masks.

about all the mileage I was going to get out of his breathing. Instead I had the rakshasa bark at her. She made a face.

"He's a gift for a friend," I said. I explained who Westin was and asked Siti what she thought of the rakshasa.

"Kasar," she said flatly. *Alus* and *kasar* are another of the great dualities in Indonesian life. To be alus is to be refined. A person who is alus speaks softly and never says the wrong thing. He always holds his head in a slightly bowed position. Moko was alus. Kasar people are loud and vulgar and have big unrefined noses. Americans, for instance.

"Let's not get into kasar," I said.

"But why a rakshasa for a nice old lady?"

Siti didn't understand about this particular old lady. "Think of it as a joke," I said. "Anyway, this particular rakshasa is only kasar on the outside. On the inside he is very alus. It is the kind of joke that nature occasionally likes to play." I was right, too. It was Karna, the sympathetic monster who supposedly died in Sri Lanka.

"You are well informed," Siti said. "If you weren't an American, I would suspect you of being alus yourself."

"Are Americans never alus?"

"Never on the outside," she said. "They are too big. Their noses, I mean."

She pretended to examine my nose very closely. This train of thought was very promising indeed. In the next row of stalls she bought a pair of shoes and I bought a kris for Jeremy. It had a nicely serpentine blade and had been aged so that you had to look carefully to see bits of new steel. It had started to rain.

"Tell me about your wife," she said. I gave her the abstract.

"I knew it."

"What did you know?"

"Divorced men have a certain look. Dieter, also, was divorced."

I was letting things take their own course. It was almost Zen-like, which is often the best way to handle these things. Anyway, what was I supposed to say about Dieter's divorce? That's too bad, maybe, or that's nice? Instead I picked a stray hair off her cheek. It was a Zen-like sort of response.

"You got the kris very cheap," she said. "That was clever of you."

"Tell me what I did."

"Waited for it to rain. When it rains the shops always reduce their prices. You were tough."

"Oh," I said.

"Americans are always tough," she said. "It is because they are afraid of being taken advantage of."

"Should I go back and pay him more?" I asked.

"Don't be silly."

Things were coming along very well indeed, and all I had to do was walk around and let them happen. It was like sleeping. We spent the rest of the morning walking around the old Dutch harbor looking at Bugis* ships and godowns† We searched in vain for accept-

---

*Bugis (pronounced "Boo-gee"). The tribe of shipbuilding pirates at whose appearance Dutch sailors shouted what was to become a staple of childhood terror: "Watch out for the Boogie man."
†Cellar warehouses for sea cargos

able boutiques. I turned her loose after lunch to widen her search perimeter while I went through the new material at the National Archives. It was amazingly dull. It suddenly struck me that the Tokyo article was trivial. All my work was trivial. I had always told myself that it was trivial, but that was just a smokescreen. It really *was* trivial.

She picked me up in one of those sports Mercedeses that not every junior ministry clerk is able to drive and we had rijsttafel at a little restaurant that was rather kasar on the outside but quite alus within. For a thoroughly Westernized woman Siti had retained a fondness for spicy foods. I was really on a roll. The kiss she gave me across the gear shift tasted like peppers and coriander.

There's nothing quite like a middle-aged fool. Before going out I had shaved for the second time and put on clean Jockey underwear. Now she was sitting in the winged chair in my hotel room eating a starfruit. I was just trying to work out the Zen-like way to close the distance when she bit off a piece of the pulp and held it out for me.

"I may not turn out to be absolutely great at this," I said. "It's been a little while."

"Dieter wasn't always great either," she said soothingly.

What I don't quite understand is how they knew I would take her home and then take a taxi back. They might reasonably have assumed that she would have to go home. I mean, this was Jakarta. She couldn't just spend the night in a strange man's hotel room. There just hadn't been time to square it with her family. But how could they have been so sure that I would turn out to be a Boy Scout? I suppose they might have been prepared to wait. It's just that I hate the thought of being so transparent. I admit that I was behaving like a kid on his first successful date. I was still tasting the peppers and coriander, and every now and then I checked to see if the perfume still clung to my cuffs and collar. I was probably whistling. The men in the van must have thought it was pretty humorous, but they didn't let it distract them from the business at hand. The one waiting at the curb wasn't even distracted when I responded to his push by mumbling "Excuse me." I am convinced that it was only my refusal to recognize a pistol that caused him to hit me. They weren't used to dealing with that level of absentmindedness. "You *are* Professor Doctor McCallum?" he said.

I agreed that I was. I don't blame him for checking. I was beginning to think that I could do without the honorific, though.

12.
Karna

Now, as soon as I recognized the pistol, I was more than happy to get into the van. I felt like apologizing, but the impulse passed. The man who was already waiting in the back had pulled a bag over my head and drawn it tight. It was one of those bags you close with a string that department stores wrap over-priced perfume in. "My face isn't that bad, really," I mumbled.

I don't think his high school and my high school shared the same joke pool. He gave the string a tug. I hoped they had considered the quantity of air a man required and the permeability of the bag. That's the kind of thing I tend to be concerned about. I could already see the headline: AMERICAN BUSINESSMAN KIDNAPPED BY ISLAMIC TERRORISTS.

Why Islamic? I don't know. I wasn't sure about businessman either. There would probably be a tussle about it at the wire-service desk, but I put my money on "businessman" over "professor" or "academic." "Businessman" is broader-based. Newspapers have to make these decisions under pressure, without benefit of market research, and I thought they would see "businessman" as a selling word. The key word, really, was "kidnapped," which they were going to have to decide whether to spell with one *p* or two. I wanted to hold it to that. I wasn't into: AMERICAN BUSINESSMAN SLAIN. I was trying to fight away the accompanying picture of a sad dead-rabbit body huddled on the side of a road. Wire-service pictures make dead bodies look so incredibly dead.

"We have some distance to travel." It was the one with the pistol, who had smacked me below the ear. "There is much to accomplish, so you will sit quietly and relax."

I felt the drawstring loosen a little, but not enough so I could talk. They drove on in silence for a little more than an hour. There were enough twists and turns that we might still have been in the suburbs. For some reason I imagined that they were on the south road toward Jogja. It's a sort of dowsing instinct I picked up as a child lying on the backseat during trips to the beach. I used to do it a lot. I believe it works a statistically significant amount of the time, although I have no hard proof. A smarter kid would have grown up to revolutionize the physics of N-dimensional spaces. Anyway, we weren't going north or west. My ears would have popped if we were heading toward the Puncak.

When we got wherever *there* was, a hand took each of my elbows and maneuvered me out of the van. They guided me up a little dirt bank, across a stone walkway, up seven steps, through two doors (I could tell from the different pressure when they maneuvered through the doors), and into an uncomfortable chair. An intense light was filtering through a pinhole in the bag. I was getting good at this, but I didn't want to make a career of it. They were quite civil, but firm about the bag.

"I'll have Iranian caviar with boiled egg on toast, plenty of toast," I said. "Then puffer fish from the Sea of Japan, well cleaned. And, Captain, please ask your men to aim for the heart."

Nothing: It wasn't going to be easy to amuse these people. I tried a different tack: "Which are you, then, Iceberg or Black Cat?"

There were footsteps, and with them a smell of fresh coffee. I have observed that the smell of fresh coffee often precedes an upturn in mood. "We are neither, Dr. McCallum. I must tell you that you are somewhat out-of-date. If you wish, you may think of us as spiritual children of Black Cat." Black Cat was the more radical of the resistance groups that had gone underground when Suharto decimated the Communists. The voice had the calculated mellowness that in Java denotes command. I was pretty sure I had not heard it in the van. He went on: "Remove the blindfold."

I waited for one of his minions to obey. I must have waited half a minute before I realized that we were alone. It took a bit of feeling around to work it out that the bag was tied with a simple bow. I gave it a tug and the bag came off with a single jerk. Across the table from me was a hairy giant. "Karna!"

"As good a name as any," the mask agreed. "Beneath the gruff exterior is a good friend. A heart of gold."

I was busy doing revisions. I had pictured myself in a spare terrorist hideout. A single intense light bulb was supposed to be hanging from the ceiling. Check, except that the light turned out to be a chandelier. The uncomfortable chair was hand-carved and would probably bring a couple of thou at Sotheby's. The room was done in basic Dutch plantation, and the table between us had once seated twenty ruddy-faced Hollanders. Karna was sitting directly across the short axis. The mask lifted my spirits. I was suddenly buying call options on my chances of getting turned loose alive. It cheered me up almost as much as the coffee, which Karna was busy pouring. "Go ahead. You won't have to worry about it keeping you awake." It also struck me as positive that he had a sense of humor.

"If you expect the university to pay handsomely for my return, you have been disserved by your Americanists," I said.

A hit. A most palpable hit. Karna actually laughed. "Oh, we know all about your business. We know that you are here to plunder our offshore resources. If blackmail were our objective, we would know exactly whom to approach. As it happens, that is not our primary concern at the moment."

"Reckon my sins are good big sins. What are they?"

"Your visit has proved to be fortuitous for us, Dr. McCallum. For both of us, actually. We would like to make you a gift."

"Right after pin the tail on the donkey. Or was it blindman's buff?"

"Latief," Karna said. Something in his tone of voice suggested that that was enough kidding around.

"Colonel A.," I said. "The Piltdown man. The missing link."

"Don't exasperate me, Professor. I am under no compulsion to treat you kindly."

"Colonel A. Latief," I said. "Aide to the General Staff Intelligence. Former hero of the People's Army. Doubled to the PKI. Implicated in the 1965 coup. His controller was Sjam. He supposedly met with General Suharto the night before the coup at a hospital where Suharto had a sick son. Later they said it was Mrs. Suharto and a sick daughter. He was supposed to be tried, but he was too sick to be brought before the Mahmillub."

"Reported to have been too sick," Karna corrected.

"I won't nitpick. After the trial he faded from the scene. Whatever he had might just as well have killed him. Too bad, because he could have cleared up a few points. I suppose one morning he woke up dead."

"You may well suppose," Karna confirmed. He was holding a folder in his hand. It must have been somewhere, but I hadn't noticed it. "We have a dictionary, if you need it."

He had certainly come prepared. Actually, I thought I was going to be able to do pretty well without the dictionary, if I could make out the script. It was handwritten, probably on some of that fine thin rag paper, but I couldn't tell for sure because it was a Xerox copy. It had a cover sheet, too: FOUND AMONG THE PRIVATE PAPERS OF A. LATIEF. Found by whom? Karna was shoving a legal pad and a pen across the table. He hadn't been kidding about a dictionary either.

I had read a few of these confessions. The one by Widjanarko would have been better if it hadn't come seven years late and a month before elections. Aidit's was supposed to have been written in a couple of hours before they put a bullet in the back of his neck. Just the same, they were very diverting. You didn't have to believe to enjoy.

"I'm not sure I can do this sort of work away from my own desk," I said. "Why don't you just trust me with this copy and I'll mail you back an opinion with the typed copy."

"The translation you are going to make is for yourself," Karna said. "You can check the facts later."

13.
Latief

Latief had gotten his start running agents against
the Dutch. He gave this in summary, beginning with
his recruitment into the wartime liberation movement. It was a sort of apology as if for bad habits he
had been unable to shake. His writing was clear and
factual, generally in Bahasa but with occasional Javanese words thrown in. It had a touch of the national linguistic schizophrenia. He used the English
convention for spelling, except for names, which were
written in the old Dutch phonetics. Thus Sukarno
was Soekarno. I noticed that when he lapsed into
Javanese, he addressed his audience by the highest
honorific, as if to say that any possible reader would
be of higher status than he, Latief.

    From the outset he was at pains to explain his
loyalties, which were to his country, the revolution,
Bung Karno, and his superior officers in the Dipo-

negoro Revolutionary Division, though not necessarily in that order. There had been one superior officer in particular, a Colonel.

Together they had defeated the Dutch and become heroes. Sukarno (or Soekarno, if you will) had become President for Life. Latief became a Colonel. The Colonel became a General. Latief was assigned as a counterintelligence officer on the Army General Staff.

They had asked him to infiltrate the PKI, making use of his friendship with a Communist organizer by the name of Sjam. This was easily done. Then Sjam had asked him to report to the Central Committee on the activities of the General Staff. This made it all the easier to carry out his military assignment.

But what had become of Latief himself? Was he an army agent among the Communists or a Communist agent among the army? Sometimes he felt that he was the secret link that held the country together. At other times he felt like a simple traitor. In his confusion, he sought counsel from his old friend the General.

The General told Latief that he had done well in seeking out counsel. He was indeed a sort of bridge between the opposing factions. The divisions among the people would not last forever. In the meantime Latief should continue exactly as he was doing, with one slight change: He should report everything he learned from both sides to his friend the General.

Things continued in this new situation until January of 1965. It was apparent by then that the divisions among the people were growing worse. Latief spoke of this to the General, who assured him that events were in the making that would resolve those differences once and for all.

In March of that year the General made a subtle addition to his brief. Beyond betraying secrets between the two groups, the General wished him to make certain small deviations in his reports, the net effect of which was to increase the animosity between the army and the PKI. When Latief complained to the General, he was told that it was necessary to bring on a crisis in order to eventually restore order. The General reminded him of his duty, but at the same time he called Latief's attention to his vulnerability if the General should withdraw his sponsorship. So Latief, already agent, double agent, and triple agent, became agent provocateur as well.

As spring passed into summer, the General's battle plan took shape. Some of it Latief was told, and some of it he was able to deduce from his long experience in intelligence.

The concept was to provoke the Army Staff into an attempt at a coup. It was a coup that could not in the end succeed, but success was not its object. In fact, the coup was never actually to take place. It was the preparation for the coup, and the setting of a date, that the General regarded as crucial. The purpose of the coup was to force the hand of Sukarno and the PKI. They were to be forced first into each other's arms for a kiss of death, then compelled into a rash counteraction, which, like the army coup, could not possibly succeed.

For this conspiracy, the role of Latief was crucial. He alone could carry exaggerated statements of

PKI plans to the Army Staff and carry back to the PKI the measures being taken by the generals. These measures were to culminate in a coup d'état, which would take place on Armed Forces Day, October 5, when a large number of troops would be present in the capital.

Latief had been skeptical. It all seemed rather convoluted, even for Indonesia. How, for instance, could the General be so sure that the Army Staff would act? He, after all, was an outsider in his post with the Strategic Reserve. The General told him to put his mind at rest. At first he was vague about the means, then he had told Latief a part of it.

The General himself had a sponsor, a clever and powerful dalang, who presumed to use the General (although like all men, the General was sure that it was he who was doing the using), and this dalang had certain means at his disposal. He could guarantee certain actions by the Army Staff. Latief gathered from certain things the General said (though politically astute, the General was no intelligence specialist) that the dalang was a foreigner. That was implied from the way in which he planned to manipulate the Army Staff.

Even more intriguing was the suggestion that this foreigner had means to influence Sukarno himself. He seemed to be in a position to funnel to Sukarno such information as would confirm the PKI intelligence about a military coup and force Sukarno into precipitate action.

Latief had done everything within his power to discover the identity of this foreign dalang. He had used the files of military intelligence to review each member of the British, Dutch, and American embassies, but his inquiries had failed. For a brief moment he told himself that the dalang was fictitious, that he was a figment the General had made up (as controllers always make up stories to reassure their agents), and then, suddenly, on September 30, it had all come to pass.

The conclusion of the confession was a morose analysis of his own stupidity—he, Latief, the agent runner who had allowed himself to be turned into the agent—and a resigned salute to the General's cleverness. Naturally, the General could not allow a man who knew what he knew to live. He hoped that the very existence of the document, in safekeeping, might stay the General's hand, but he did not doubt that the General would find this, too, a small obstacle. He spoke of the measuring of ends and means and the pangs of conscience. Being a thorough man, trained in intelligence work, he attached an appendix listing the dates of meetings of which he had kept a detailed record. He also included his estimate of time windows in which the General must have met with his own dalang.

14.
Riddle

The drive back into Jakarta felt like less than an hour. Return trips always seem shorter because you know the way. I also had plenty to think about. There was no reason on earth to believe that the Latief confession was genuine. Why had it turned up after all these years, and how had Karna got his hands on it? Karna wasn't talking. There was a certain logic to his approach. In his own hands the document was worthless. It would be like a Jew turning up with a confession by the man who actually started the Reichstag fire. Naturally that wouldn't do. But if a neutral expert validated it ... What I had wanted to know was, how could they be so sure I would authenticate it, even if I decided it was genuine? It could, after all, be most damaging to my country. "The jaws of the crocodile always snap," Karna said.

"It is the nature of the beast. The crocodile doesn't stop to ask whose leg is in his mouth."

They dumped me off a little unceremoniously, I thought, for a newfound friend and ally. Maybe I was just off form after all those hours of translating. They say that intense close-focus work disorients your ability to function in a large visual spatial frame. Somewhere along the way I had dulled my skills for stepping over curbs with a sack over my head.

I heard giggles and reached up to untie the bow around my neck. This time the bastard had done it in some kind of sailor hitch. The van was in Surabaya by the time I got it untied. The cheeky bastards had dropped me off smack in front of Merdeka Palace. I was surrounded by a gaggle of schoolchildren in their blue and white uniforms. Very funny, ha-ha. A pinch-faced schoolmarm was trying to get them back into ranks, while I seemed to have set them off on the idea of blindman's buff. Schoolteachers are the same everywhere.

The taxi to the hotel took about five minutes. I had just time to shower and shave and give the financials a run through in the *Straits Times*. Boy, was I going to do some sleeping one of these days. Indoil was up another ⅞. Tidelands was down ⅛ at 27⅜. Not much of a move, but everything in the right direction is all to the good. The rest of the market was narrowly mixed.

Siti had obviously slept like a winter bear. I had to remember that her last relevant experience had been sex. Divergent living had created a gap between us. "You look like hell," she said.

"Thanks," I said. I agreed absolutely. "You seemed to think I looked okay yesterday."

"I tried to call you when I got home."

"What can I say?" I said. What could I say? "I got lucky. When I got into the elevator, there was this blonde. These professor types are insatiable, you know."

"I kept on calling for more than an hour."

She gave a little pout. "Have you ever heard the one about the three smudges?" I asked.

"What three smudges are these? What does this have to do with last night?"

"It's a riddle," I said. "Once upon a time there was this old sultan. The sultan had three sons. He had decided to give his sultanate to the smartest son."

"I still don't see what the smartest son has to do with last night."

"But the sultan had to find out which son was the smartest. So he locked all three sons in a closed room. He put a smudge of water-buffalo dung on each son's forehead."

"Is this a vulgar story? If it is vulgar, I don't want to hear it."

"Very well, then, not water-buffalo dung, camel dung. Or ashes, if you prefer." She smiled in spite of herself. I wondered if it was hard to get good orthodontic work in Jakarta. "So the sultan instructs each son that he is to raise his hand as soon as he sees a smudge. As soon as he knows *with certainty* whether his own forehead contains a smudge, he is to drop his hand. When the light comes on in the room, all three hands go up. After a split second delay, the hand of the smartest son goes down again. He wins the kingdom, eats many rijsttafels, and becomes the ancestor of Hamengku Buwono." Hamengku Buwono is the present Sultan of Jogja. He is best known for tooling around Jakarta in a sports car. "But how did the smart son know *for certain* that his forehead contained a smudge?"

The pout returned. "You are trying to make me feel unintelligent."

"Quite the contrary. I am trying to help you repeat the smart son's legendary feat."

"How did he know?"

"Simple. If his own forehead had contained no smudge, even the dull brothers would have been able to know *with certainty* that their foreheads contained smudges. When they did not lower their hands, he knew it was safe to lower his."

"A very clever riddle," Siti said. "Your university must be very proud to have such a man."

"But that's not the riddle," I said. "The riddle is, what do we mean when we say 'with certainty'? Was the smart son's knowledge of a logical or psychological nature? And was the answer really worth a sultanate?"

"Now you are asking an Indonesian riddle. You should put it to Moko. He will give you an answer with six more questions and a crocodile. This afternoon you will have your opportunity."

"He has an answer on the oil tracts?"

"The business has been discussed at the ministry. There is a final meeting this morning. We are to be at the ministry at two."

"And what shall we do with the morning?"

"I would like to discover the truth about professor types," she said. "The word 'insatiable' has been used."

I was surprised at how fast things were moving. I didn't trust Moko's smile and hearty handshake—an Indonesian firing squad would smile and ask how they could be of service—but he seemed to be saying that the ministry accepted the terms Crockett offered. I went over them point by point and there was no doubt about it. Crockett was getting exactly what he wanted, lock, stock, and a lifting reduction of several million barrels.

The virtue of that smiling poker face is that it just lulls you right to sleep. A part of you just switches off. By the time I was really sure he meant yes, Moko had lit up a large Dutch cigar and used it as a springboard for talking about his studies in Holland. He had gone there to study engineering. "Civil engineering, or else geology. After one semester I switched to economics. I had learned that the engineers end up working for the economists. It took me longer to learn who the economists work for."

"The essence of education," I said, "is learning that the people who believe that the important things are contained in books end up hewing wood and drawing water or teaching at universities."

"The economics I learned in the Netherlands was perfectly useless here," Moko went on. "Except as a credential, of course. I hung the certificate up on the wall. It helped convince people when I told them to put the jam on the top side of the bread. It's true, though, that I learned something of the world. We have a saying in central Java that a crocodile has its radius. Its strength is measured by the circle within which another creature dares not approach."

"Sphere of influence," I suggested.

"Precisely. I grew up believing that Indonesia was a large crocodile, but Holland taught me different. For a holiday some friends and I rented an automobile and drove to every major city just to show it could be done. It can. And yet when I was a boy, these Dutchmen gave commands that were carried out in Jakarta. As crocodiles, they were doing something right."

"So you came back and joined KAPPI."

Moko shrugged and relit his cigar. The shrug did not say that I was wrong, but it said that only an American would try to draw a single moral from a story. The story was about the unreliability of childhood impressions and the ubiquity of crocodiles. It forgave the Dutch, who were after all only doing their job as crocodiles. It was about self-deception and the unexpected complexity of the world. And like every crocodile story, it was also a diversion, serving to distract my attention while a dog failed to bark.

He left it to Siti to see me off.

"I'll write you letters," she said in the Mercedes. She had it centered very squarely between the two No Parking signs.

"No. No letters."

"But the telephone hours are all wrong, and besides, it's so expensive. The things I want to say you can't put on a telex. In Jakarta they won't let you."

"They won't let you anywhere," I said. "No tel-exes, no telegrams."

"Then what?"

"I once bought my son an expensive dog," I said. "The man who sold it loved that dog. He warned me not to keep any Dial soap in the house, because if it was there, the dog would eat it, and once he ate it nothing you could do would save it. No antidote. And I wasn't supposed to go calling him to tell him how the dog was doing. He didn't want to hear from me. If something happened to that dog, he didn't want to know. Don't start to cry. Let today be the first day of your adult life."

"You and Moko should go into business to-gether. You make a fine pair. Cute little stories and hearts of stone."

That was when it hit me. Gus Friedler did an article about it. The remarkable thing was the reg-ularity of it. It amounted to a sort of fee schedule of skims and bribes and kickbacks. "The Appanage System in Indonesian Civil Service." It provided a stable, predictable basis on which to transact busi-ness. It eliminated the curse of the idiosyncratic free-lancer.

Moko and I were old chums, but this was an area where chumship just didn't figure. He had a budget to meet. In a deal like this, there were layers and layers of bureaucrats, from the ministry clerks who stamped the papers to the foremen who would now wear hats with Emerald Crockett written on them. Supervisors. Inspectors. How was he going to meet their share of the take, and he and I not even having discussed the basic kickback? Something was very amiss here. I felt like I had failed at my job and Siti was trailing along at high pout.

Security let me get about twenty yards beyond the arch before they came running up to grab my elbows. I had my translation of the Latief confession folded into the side compartment of my shaving kit, but all that would do in the case of a search was reveal that I intended to hide it. I have difficulty understanding when several people talk rapidly in Bahasa, and all I really knew was that they were pointing to my carry-on bag. It was Siti who understood and sent for my suitcase, which luckily had not yet been loaded into the handling modules. The three of them and Siti watched with satisfaction as I removed Jeremy's kris from the carry-on and placed it in the middle of an embarrassing jumble of shirts. No one was going to hijack this flight at knifepoint. They let Siti go to the gate, however. There was just no stopping her. I gave her a peck on the cheek.

"The best you can come up with?" she said.

I reminded her of the banyan tree. A woman whose husband went away to war was besieged by lovers, who told her he had been killed. When she prayed to see him, the gods turned her into the banyan tree. They turned her husband into the crow, which sits in the banyan branches. "You wouldn't be happy as a tree," I said.

"Men are bastards," she said. "The woman who made you like this should have her eyes scratched out."

"I'll tell you one more story," I said. The flight attendant was gesturing pointedly. "I was once at

Borobudur with a great Indonesian anthropologist. I asked him why they had let it fall into ruin and be covered by jungle. Do you know what he said?"

She shook her head.

"He just shrugged. He showed me a wild orchid. Gone tomorrow, here forever, he said. It's the temples that always fall apart. Let what happened be like the orchid."

She pulled away from the embrace. "Bastard," she said. "When we made love you were thinking of your wife."

15.
Quitter

For a man who had probably just gone over the billion mark, Crockett didn't seem that excited. I told myself that was probably the precise quality that got you the first half billion to play with. He did ask for a few details. After all, he paid for the plane ticket.

"The effective date on the lifting reduction?"

I told him.

"You see. That's the way those buggers negotiate with you. If the deal goes through in a hurry, I'll be out of pocket for ten or eleven months. Hell, I'll have to rent storage capacity. I better get a note out on it. Maybe I can dump some of it on Sohio to make up their underlift from Prudhoe Bay."

"I hope I didn't negotiate it wrong." I was really waiting for him to ask about the kickbacks; I was nervous about that one.

"Wrong? Hell, I'm lucky they didn't hold out for

half the length of the contract. It's just that no deal is ever quite as good as it looks before the fine print." He thought over this new insight. "What I suppose I could do is drag out the offer for Indoil and try to structure the deal so I stick the present owners with the loss." I could see the idea growing on him. "Yep, that's it. I'll hold my tender offer back, and, better yet, I'll play some games with the final settlement date. I may not even start buying the stock for a few weeks."

"You mean you haven't started yet?" I tried to be casual.

"Hell, no." I thought I saw his eyes narrow. "Couldn't do that before I got the go-ahead from friend Moko. Now could I?"

"But your associates could."

"Now, boy, that wouldn't make a lick of sense. You use associates to stay shy of the Feds and their reporting rules, not to make money at your own expense for everybody's cousins and nephews." As he talked he looked me up and down, as if I might have unsuspected qualities. I was half-tempted to warn him that the stock was already going up, but I thought better of it. A man in his position could afford a *Wall Street Journal* of his own. "That's why you're not in the company-busting end of it," he said with finality. "You just leave that end of it to me and watch the newspapers."

"I'll do that," I said. It was an exit line. My end of it had been quite enough.

Laura Westin seemed considerably more impressed with me. They didn't have the *Journal* on the flight out of Dallas, but *The New York Times*, for all its editorial content, tends to be accurate in its financial quotes. Indoil was up (a quarter) for the sixth straight session, and Tidelands was off another five eighths.

"I'm beginning to think you're really onto something," Westin conceded.

"Do I ever give you a bad tip?"

She ignored the remark. Westin saw herself primarily as needler, not needlee. "At this rate I am going to owe you a dinner when I cover."

"Cover today and you can book Perroquet for the weekend."

"Oh, no," she said sharply. "Don't be premature. You never close a winning position. I think I'll just put in a stop a point or two above the market. You know what they say: Cut your losses and let your winners ride."

"That's very clever," I said. "I should take that kind of advice to heart."

"Besides, your friend Mr. Crockett is going to be buying a great deal more Indoil. When it becomes apparent to everyone, it's Tidelands straight down the tubes."

"For your information," I said, "Mr. Crockett has yet to buy *any* Indoil."

That seemed to take some drinking in. She looked at me as if I were insane, and only a few minutes ago I had been so wise. I thought I should explain.

"You see, we corporate barracudas delay our buying to the proper moment because of SEC rules. To say nothing of certain other factors which I am not at liberty to divulge. Now if you could ring Max

Edel at the library, there is a research task we have to get on with."

"How very odd!" she said. "And the stock showing such good relative strength."

She took her time ringing Max, which is her way of saying that she does that kind of task out of pure personal affection and not because she regards it as part of her job. She filled the interval by lowering her glasses to the middle of her nose. It's a gesture that in Laura Westin means that she is looking at the hidden heart of things with an eye that requires no glasses. She gave me the same response when I told her I also needed ten years' back reports of Tech Systems.

Max Edel lives in a little cubicle to the rear of the rare-book room, and I say lives advisedly. He has a cot, and I have caught him with a closet door open revealing several changes of clothes, including a tux. Although his official title is Curator of Rare Books, he is in reality a special resource to the reference section of the library. A lot of the things Max is expert on are not indexed in *Britannica*. Give him a subject, no matter how arcane, and he can generate a bibliography on it. I don't know how he does it, but it has to be with databases and the two, count 'em two, computers in his cubicle. I explained my problem.

"What you really need is to access the archives of the intelligence agencies," he said.

"Don't I know it," I agreed. "Your computers won't do that, will they?"

"Then again, if the Franks had kept good records, it would have put all those medievalists out of work." That's how Max answers simple questions. His hands were already on the keyboard.

You didn't have to give Max much. Latief, if you believed in him, had done a big chunk of the legwork. And you had to believe in him. The man we were looking for had not worked out of an embassy slot. That was a big head start. Somewhere, on an off-the-books budget line, there was an entry that would stick out like a sore thumb. We had to believe that. It was just enough to start with.

The thing was, I knew what I was looking for. That's what separates the real scholar from the one who may as well be reading the library from Aa to Zygote. I mean, it's always going to come out of left field, but it's going to come out of left field in a certain *way*. Don't press me on it, or I'll end up using words like creativity and imagination. There's also thine ancient sacrifice, an iron butt. The trick in the beginning, as Max said, is to be *wantonly* inclusive. He had once helped a historian change the view of the Battle of Gettysburg with a line from a child's picture history; it had drawn on a private family memoir. That, Max and I agreed, is the way it always comes in, after you have pumped through the short list of one hundred and sixty sources, most of them books, more than half of then unindexed, the lazy bastards. When I left, I had six crates of them, good for five trips to the car, which I couldn't get any closer than fifty yards to the library and another thirty to my front door, so don't ever say legwork wasn't a part of it. Max checked them out himself, standing at the console with his little electronic beeper and reminding me that they had due dates just like any other books. He was well acquainted with my personal and library habits.

Actually, the books were a comfort in the empty house. I had kept it when Helen left because the low mortgage made it cheaper than an apartment (she had made me buy just before the run-up in rates). That's what I told people. The real reason was that with the insomnia and all I didn't have the energy to move. I had thirty, maybe forty years left, and I was going to spend 2 to 3 percent of it on a move? I simply closed off a couple of rooms like chapters of my life.

There were bills to sort through and a couple of journals that for some reason always come to my home address. I moved the crates to my study, took out the top one, and drank in the dusty, mildewy smell. This was what it was to be an intellectual. There were only about sixteen million words contained in those crates, let's say a hundred and fifty thousand paragraphs, and I was lucky to find the paragraph I wanted on Sunday evening:

> My replacement on the grain investigation had been dispatched from Langley to take over the AID program. "Charles Francis" was an old hand, having been around for the Sumatra fiasco of 1958. He seemed a trifle overqualified for the job, and in fact he spent most of his time hobnobbing with the Jakarta brass and chums like the head of Socony-Vacuum up in Palembang.

It was on page 437 of *I Quit,* a confessional masterpiece by one Tommy Hamer, who had indeed done the one thing Grampa Jack said winners never do (and those who do it never win). He hadn't either. It had sold about six hundred copies, half to libraries and the other half to the KGB. About the only thing I can say in his behalf is that he had the sense of craft to put together an index. Maybe he had his own Laura Westin. As none other than Max Edel said, the cross-reference is one of the ten greatest human inventions. Without indexes, though, the connections are greatly less obvious:

Kirby, Fred: OSS ties, 131; Italian elections of 1948, 131; and James Angleton, 132; Renville Agreement, 176; Burma Operation (*see also* Li Mi), 212; with Kermit Roosevelt in Tehran (*see also* Pahlavi, Mohammad Reza, Shahanshah), 245; with Lansdale in Manila (*see* Magsaysay, Ramon), 318; Sumatra (*see* Sumatran colonels), 388, *also* footnote, 521; labor and student organizations, 431; at FE-5, 441ff.

What I did then was call the archives department at State and explain that I needed some old rosters to fill in gaps for a monograph I was doing on career-advancement patterns since Wristonization.* We chatted for a while about the relative merits of assignments in the political and economic cones, but after a while I admitted to her that what I was

*The Wriston study in the early 1950s led to the professionalization of the Foreign Service.

really hot after was the stuff that happened to career FSOs when they got sidetracked into programs. I told her not to mention it, that a fellow out at San Diego State was trying to scoop me.

"Confidentially, getting sent to the boondocks to run a program can really mess up your career," I said.

"Yes, but aren't a lot of those people *reserve* officers?"

She was right on top of things. "That's true," I said, "but that just makes it all the more telling for a career man."

She was a pip and got those rosters right out to me. I only felt slightly guilty as a taxpayer for feeling it necessary to ask for so many more than I actually needed. It was there, okay, Foreign Service Reserve and all. They hadn't wised up on that until Agee blew the entire Latin American division by office numbers and embassy phone books.

A.I.D. COORD COLE, FRANCIS S.K. FSR
9/29/64–3/20/67

If the Russians didn't have the complete batting order, they weren't playing with a full deck. But then so many people weren't in this business.

16.
Smith, Brown, and Robinson

When I came up for air, Indoil had dropped five eighths and then another seven eighths. I asked Laura Westin if she had seen it, and she certainly had.

"What are you going to do?" It took me completely by surprise. "What did Sorel do? Cover?"

"My goodness no. Mr. Sorel was talking about shorting more."

"Glutton for punishment," I said. "Did it trigger your stop?"

"Tut. Mr. Sorel and I managed to get through to the specialist at the post. Merrill had just dropped it from an OKAY TO BUY on a price basis. The Merrill analyst said the current price contained unwarranted takeover speculation."

"And that didn't worry you?"

She used her best old-maidish voice. "I dropped

my stop on Tidelands to twenty-seven and a half. If you check, you'll see that it's been holding at twenty-six and seven eighths. To win at this game, you have to have intestinal *fortitude*."

I liked that. I liked the way she put intestinal fortitude in italics. My mail had contained a notice from the library.

"What's this from the library? I checked these books out two days ago and they already want them back?"

"I'm going to organize a course in remedial reading for tenured professors," she said. "If you look beyond your name, the slip explains that another patron has requested the books. The library is revoking your three-month privileges and asking for a regular two-week return."

I counted on Laura Westin to be up on that kind of thing. The request was for speed-up return of four books, and the Hamer book was one of them.

"Have you ever done the Smith-Brown-Robinson puzzle?" I asked Westin.

"I just type and take telephone messages," she said. "I'm not even required to make coffee, send off for annual reports, or know the library regulations."

"They're the kind of puzzle you work on in intelligence analysis."

"Is that what you did in the war, Daddy?"

"Let's say Smith, Brown, and Robinson are a Stoker, a Driver, a Guard, and a Porter . . ."

"They don't have Stokers anymore," Westin chirped. "I don't believe they do anyway. And darn few Porters."

"Okay, not a Porter. Let's say a Covert Operative. And not in any order. And then let's say each man wears either a red or a blue or a black or a green shirt."

"I've noticed that you have a thing for pale blue. I think someone must have told you it goes with your eyes."

"Okay, then." Classical tactical doctrine says it is best to ride out this kind of volley without reply. "Then let's say that the Driver beats Brown at racquetball. And it is also well known that the Guards go golfing together on Thursdays with the men in the black and green shirts."

"The bit about Thursdays is a red herring," Westin said instantly. I noticed, however, that she was jotting on a note pad. "And who ever heard of a black shirt outside of Los Angeles?"

"There was Mussolini," I said. "But while we're on the subject, there's a call I'd like you to make for me. My fingers did the walking, but it'll be more impressive if my secretary comes on first."

While she dialed I went on with the story. "Robinson and your improbable Porter did not get along with the man in the green shirt, who was not the Covert Operative," I continued. "Covert Operatives always wear red shirts."

"I expect green might do more for your eyes than sickly blue," she said. She was dialing with the eraser end. "It can't be solved with the available information."

It was another of those declarative questions.

"Oh, I think it almost can," I said.

Hamer was a hard man to talk to. He was one of those men who are just so busy, whatever you have to say can't possibly be as important as their activity at the moment. I started out by telling him that I was doing a monograph on personnel attrition in federal agencies; I went on for a while about the relative merits of statistical and anecdotal data, how hard it was to get good anecdotal, but when that didn't cut any ice, I told him I had to talk to him about Francis Kirby Cole, and that I would be in Los Angeles tomorrow afternoon. That finally got his attention.

I asked Westin to book me to L.A.

"And give up my priority work on the puzzle?"

"I first solved it when I was eight," I said. That got her to call the airline.

The girl at the reserve desk explained that she had helped the two men herself. No, she hadn't stopped to think it was odd that *two* men were looking for books. They were looking for six, of which the catalog had four. No, they didn't want her to order the other two on the sharing agreement. But for the four that were checked out, they wondered for how long and to whom. It had seemed important to them. She had thought Max would have wanted her to be helpful. Once she told them, they had just shrugged and said, oh, well. She had offered to put the books on early recall, but they had said, repeat, never mind. Still, a lot of people say that kind of thing and then come back the very next day, as if a professor is going to remember to turn his books in three months early. It was worth a probe. She had taken a little initiative and sent me the notices. She liked to be helpful, she really did. There was more, but I wasn't listening carefully. I was busy wondering if they were the same two men who had spent the past two evenings sitting two houses down on my block in their dingy, dusty, beat-up Buick.

17.
Danauer

The *L.A. Times* proved a wealth of useful information. The Lakers were still on a streak. Abdul-Jabbar was coming into mid-season form, and Magic had a hot hand. Some charity group wanted to cite Sinatra for his service to the elderly. Sunshine was expected. Indoil had recovered a half point on good volume. I had taken the ticket out of my SEAAAC travel account, which had $1,887.54 in it. I thought it was fair since Crockett had paid for the Jakarta trip, but it was going to provide the grant administrator with some pretty interesting reading.

The third time I tried my key it turned out to be my very own Alamo Rent A Car. I drove the freeway with the kind of abandon one reserves for the use of well-broken-in equipment for which others are required to do the maintenance. My mind was *elsewhere*, which is probably the very best state for rapid lane changes. High alpha-particle emission, good Zen-like eye/hand.

Los Angeles was going to help me clear up a great deal. I had this old notion of my own about the 1965 coup, along with a confession that was almost inhumanly convenient. Hamer could probably clear it all up. He was also the kind of guy who could tell you how a DDA report got itself used for a DDO operation. Danauer was strictly a courtesy call.

His bungalow was at the end of a cul-de-sac in Pacific Hills. It looked like it just might have a view of Blue Pacific. I was already totting up the amount of frontage times seventeen zillion when I remembered that the Santa Monica Institute had bought up a few dozen lots sometime in the Late Middle Ages. They leased them out to senior associates for a song, including emeriti, which was the closest the institute ever came to using the word *retired*. Lucky Danauer, although I couldn't quite picture him in L.A. Where he belonged was strictly the *philosophenweg*, where they didn't even have motorcycles, much less sports cars, although I wouldn't be surprised if the *jungen* got a motorcycle up it every now and then. There certainly was a sports car in his driveway, and if it wasn't a Jaguar they had better check who was using their logo on a cheap knockoff. It wasn't a cheap knockoff. I was curious to see if Danauer still looked like the before of the professor in *Der Blaue Engel* or if he had taken to Bermuda shorts.

I was met at the door by Mrs. D., who hedged her greeting. "Visitors are good for Friedrich, even if he doesn't always know it." She was an Indonesian beauty a good twenty years younger than Danauer, and some people in Chicago had said he kept her under wraps out of simple prudence, although I personally suspected it was out of consideration for senior faculty unfamiliar with Indonesians, who didn't know whether they had to lay off Negro stories or Chinaman stories.

Danauer himself appeared in her wake holding up his soiled hands like a surgeon who has just scrubbed. He had been gardening. He did the hand scrubbing in a large laundry sink with the kind of thoroughness impolite people call Prussian. He made coffee the same way, grinding the beans and then setting the pot on the stove with movements that were at once awkward and precise.

"We will now have coffee and a treat," he said. "And then you will explain to me why you did this outlandish thing."

Tien Danauer returned with two tall glasses of gula melaka. I noticed that Danauer gardened in gray denims, a white shirt, and high-laced German walking shoes. He called Tien "my dear" and maneuvered her about the room by touching her at the elbows with the same loose-armed awkwardness he had applied to the coffee grinder. It was an old Danauer trick, a parody of the detached, unworldly professor holding coffee, girl, and jazz record at arm's length. I didn't buy it entirely, but it was certainly preferable to belching loudly and saying, hey, ain't this the life.

"Keeping up is now my chief professional responsibility," he said as Tien discreetly departed. "They sent me your article. I thought I was the one who was supposed to be senile."

That's the trouble with this lingan-dorgan business. Seeing an old teacher is like a first legal drink. You remember trying to cheat, and he remembers all the others he caught cheating. You just can't ever really be equals.

"I just never accepted that the case was closed," I assayed. "Maybe I was stupid."

"Oh, for God's sake." He looked at me like a freshman who has come in to argue against his own exam paper. "Didn't the trials settle it?"

"People lie at show trials," I argued. "You've lived in the twentieth century."

"People lie at show trials, but they have a particular way of lying. A good lie must adhere in certain aspects to the truth. A patient and clever man can often find out a great deal from a sufficiently detailed lie. Sometimes, more than from the truth."

"The Reds did it, case closed."

"Oh, Keith," he gave a sort of moan. "And the rest of your work was going so well. Such a promising career. Let it drop and maybe the profession will have you back. In time they will. The work on oil is quite solid. Go on, and you will become a cruel story they tell to graduate students. You'll end up like me, a garnish in an institute of computer scholars and spies."

"Oren Lewes," I said. "Speaking of. Chief analyst at the Southeast Asia desk. One of the good spies. The kind they talk about when they recruit at the foreign-language departments."

"What about him?"

"Didn't you work for him? Was he the one who signed off on your retainer?"

"Technically I'm not supposed to discuss this," Danauer said.

"You did work with Lewes. You had no problems?"

"A small disagreement once over billed expenses. I can't complain. They treated me well. Why this sudden interest in Lewes?"

I told him my story about the Malaysian tin. For some reason I didn't mention the TSY report. "I thought you might have some insight," I said. "As a matter of fact, I thought you might have been the one who recommended me to Lewes."

Danauer paused to consider this. "It's possible. It's entirely possible I mentioned your name. They did occasionally ask for referrals."

Tien Danauer tiptoed into the room and whispered something to her husband. With a shrug that said he had only been choosing his moment, he invited me to lunch. I declined twice and accepted. It's because of these little rituals that people manage to get along even as well as they do.

It was nice to see Danauer served with such devotion. A precise half cup of espresso, careful portions of veal laboriously cleaned. And for lunch. Lunch. For a man who had watched his father literally dragged from the lectern in Heidelberg, who had never been able to finish his degree, Danauer had done all right with himself.

The same sun that bathed Papeete and Denpasar came through Danauer's panorama on the Pacific. He offered me a cigar, accepted my refusal, and lit one for himself. "You're quite right. They're just as bad as the other things, and even nastier. Lucky for me I'm at a point where it doesn't make any difference." He took a deep puff. "Now tell me that you are going to give up this nonsense."

Beneath the Curt Jurgens parody he watched me shrewdly. I changed my mind about mentioning Latief.

"You aren't disturbed when the explanations remain so contradictory?"

"It's the real world, Keith. Ask three witnesses to describe an auto accident. Do you recall our first conversation on this subject?"

"I was young then," I apologized.

"Oh, but you were right," he said. "There is a book about it by a T. S. Kuhn. At any given time, Kuhn says, there is a single best theory about the world. Gradually contradictory evidence builds up. Anomalies, he calls them. Pretty soon there is unbearable tension in the people who believe the old theory. They have a sort of nervous breakdown. Then along comes an Einstein—that's what you insisted you were, Keith—unburdened by the errors of conventional wisdom. This Einstein sets things right. He makes the new facts fit. He restores sanity. You follow?"

I nodded.

"But here's the point: A new theory does not succeed because everyone instantly accepts it. Far from it. The old generation tried to wipe Einstein out. It's a matter of personal investment in a vision of the world. Old men go down to the grave fighting for their view of things. The new theory doesn't prevail until they are replaced in the university chairs. When they die out." It seemed to remind him of something. "I suppose you read about Gus Friedler. He died suddenly over the weekend. Heart attack. It was in the *New York Times* obits."

And so it was. Danauer showed it to me in his own home copy.

18.
Darwin to DNA to Dead Man

Hamer may have been the key to this, but I couldn't get Big Gus Friedler out of my mind. Big Gus, who liked to laugh and swear and drink sake or bakyang or rice wine or whatever he could get his hands on and who had once taken me to eat turtle saté cooked in sandpits on the beach. Big Gus who could appreciate native girls and was as nuts about his kids as I was about Jeremy. Who had gotten drunk enough over letting me down to make indiscreet telephone calls in bars.

I was beginning to know something. I had evidence, too. The trouble is that there are two kinds of evidence. There is fossil evidence, and then there is actually knowing how the thing works. Darwin kept noticing all these skeletons and it occurred to him that something was going on, but it wasn't until

Francis Crick came along that we knew how it really worked. That was what I had to know.

I turned off Highway 42 and started looking for street signs in a place called Fullerton. Hamer's neighborhood wasn't as ritzy as Danauer's had been, and you couldn't have seen water without standing on a space needle. What it had was a kind of homogenized anonymity for accountants with roots in Kansas and ex-spies who hadn't even managed to pop off successfully. It gave me the sort of creeps that the realms of failure are supposed to impart.

Hamer's house looked like something out of the small-town Middle West, and I suppose that's what he saw in it. There was a fence on each side, both wooden but one made of vertical stakes and the other of horizontal planks. The local zoning laws say which side the owner is responsible for, but I couldn't guess whether the newer one, vertical stakes, would have been Hamer's taste. The gate to the backyard was in an altogether different style, the same as informed the low white pickets that pretended to protect the front flower beds from dogs. No dogs were in evidence, but neither were there any flowers. The house was going to cost him $5,000 worth of painting soon, less if he did it himself, or as Helen would have said, a lot more later.

Our appointment was for two-thirty, allowing me five minutes to scout the architecture. There were no lights on, upstairs or down, and no signs of activity. I knocked for about five minutes before letting the wave of discouragement break over me. No decent fellow, I thought, would allow a body to fly two thousand miles to be stood up. A thin shred of hope said he would be in the backyard, doing chores. Carpentry, I thought; he was the sort of man who would be a Saturday backyard carpenter. I would find a deck of the kind that they can teach you to build in Time-Life Books.

There wasn't a deck, but there was a closed-in screen porch, and at first I thought he had locked up a dog in it. I opened the screen door cautiously. Hamer's body was slumped neatly against the back door. As there were no visible wounds, I assumed that he was another victim of those unexpected heart attacks that occasionally overtake healthy men in his occupation. I had no inclination to examine closely, but I touched a cold hand and cheek and guessed that he had been dead for at least twenty-four hours, or since shortly after my telephone call. The more precise answer would have to come from the Oriental fellow who reads the forensic reports on all the spectacular L.A. murders, Tate and so on. The face was puffy and swollen, though whether from long and devoted alcoholism or some effect of sudden death I had no idea. Maybe thirty-six hours, I revised my estimate, which would have put it close to the phone call indeed. In another thirty-six the neighbors would have to send someone to check. I made it as far as the cement birdbath before throwing up.

The fossil evidence was getting fresher, all right.

When I got to the gate, I noticed the car with the two men parked halfway up the block. It was the same car that had been parked across from my house. Not the actual same one, of course, but the generic same—dents, old model, dusty license. This time an

Oldsmobile. What I did then was mostly instinctive. I let out with a "Yoo-hoo, Tommy," as if he might be in an upstairs toilet or busy insulating his attic. Then I went back to the front door one more time and yoo-hooed a couple more times. I listened for an answer and gave a very theatrical shrug. Then I quickly stole his mail.

It seemed like the kind of thing Marlowe or Lew Archer might have done. It was certainly the only thing the two men in the car hadn't gone over at leisure. The postman had been packing up at the corner when I arrived. I walked very purposefully to my car, the same way you walk across an open stage to get a diploma or an award, and was relieved that the shaking of my hand did not prevent it from starting. I was even more relieved when the Oldsmobile didn't pull out behind me.

For an ex-spy Hamer turned out to get a pretty standard batch of mail. Publishers' Clearing House wanted to make him rich. A local Cadillac dealer sent him personal, confidential notice of a big saving they were willing to give favored clients. American Express sent him a bill with a one-month carryover. A forwarded letter from Taipei, which addressed him as Manager, Pacific Trading, Inc., reminded him of payment due for sixty each authentic Japanese silk kimonos.

I looked it up in the Yellow Pages. Pacific Trading listed both Hamer's home numbers and a Venice address, and I followed that one to a dingy backstreet warehouse. It was what Marlowe would have done. Whatever Pacific Trading was, it wasn't a boutique. The doors were padlocked in a manner that was at least half serious. I should have learned my lesson about walking around to the back of things, but I am more a thorough learner than a fast one. There wasn't much to see through the back window except a few cardboard boxes and bits of broken glass. One of the pieces of cardboard had a modernistic block-letter TS logo stenciled onto it.

There was a truck dock with a little enclosed office to house a shipping clerk—as good a function for the "manager" as anything I could think of. From what you could see through the windows, very little else went on at Pacific Trading except for loading and unloading. The office had been abandoned, but not padlocked. The desk had been cleaned in a hurry, leaving paper clips, calendar, pencils, and two pads of invoices, one to Pacific Trading (Export/Import: Los Angeles—Manila—Jakarta) and the other to FSC Export/Import: Los Angeles—Oakland—Singapore—Jakarta.

The two men would have been right on top of me if it hadn't been for the couple playing Man from Rio under the loading dock. The first thing I heard was a young woman's voice saying "Hey, Bobby, what the hell?"

They were creeping up like a couple of proper voyeurs, all right. Bobby and his lady came bolting out from under the dock doing a kind of Chaplin-esque zipping-up routine, and I picked up the exchange of glances between the two men. One had a crewcut and the other one an exaggerated version of what used to be called a Princeton, and they ran about six two and two-ten or so, just too small for NFL linebackers and a little too pudgy and Caucasoid to make good heavyweights. Picture aging FBI agents, which in fact was one thought that crossed my mind. Or just picture mean country boys who look like they eat railroad spikes for breakfast.

"It's the fucking cops," said Bobby's girl.

"The fuck they are," Bobby said. I realized that the jeans and T-shirt rounded out his wardrobe.

I was inclined to agree with Bobby. I gave another little shrug. Under stress you fall back on old standbys.

"Let's go, kids," I said. The men exchanged another look, and it was just enough head-start time for my bolt to the car. I passed their Oldsmobile again and commenced the crazy zigzag routine that had been my technique for hide-and-seek games when I was a kid. I did a lot of aimless dashing around city streets and freeways, trying to have a firm physical sense that I had lost them, yet knowing all the while that when all was said and done I still had to end up at home free. Home free was LAX. I told myself that they weren't really after me, who was I to them? If I just got on my plane and got out of town, they would let me be. I dropped off the car, took the Alamo bus, and made the gate with two minutes to spare. There were no brick-eating hulks in the queue. I was in the clear for four hours or two thousand nautical miles. I had already come to the conclusion that there are worse things than February Chicago weather.

19.
Semiotics to Hermeneutics to Sex

What they had done to my poor old house I don't even want to talk about. There is a Graham Greene story that tells it all about a house and a gang of hoodlum teenagers. It wasn't burglars. I could see that right off. I have been burglarized before, and although it is enough to restore your support for capital punishment, this was something different entirely. A burglar doesn't mind throwing your possessions all over the floor, starting with the bottom drawers first and discarding what doesn't catch his fancy without too much regard for the sensibilities of the cleaning lady. I even imagine there are burglars who tap walls and probe loose plaster in the back of closets, especially if they find two weeks' mail neatly stacked on the hallstand.

But this was another thing. When the pace of events in my life slowed down, I was going to have to retile the bathroom shower and half the floor, reinsulate the attic and crawl space, plus seal it off again, redo all the kitchen cabinets, replace books and bookcases, reupholster furniture, reframe pictures and paintings, and sort through what had been boxes of mementos, personal records, and old toys in the basement storeroom. This would be after I had gotten rid of the odor of spoiled food. I mean, who would hide anything between layers of frozen Swanson dinners or in refrigerator gratings? And wouldn't you think that men with time to do all that could have spared just a couple of seconds to replug the thing?

Then there were the soft places where walls had been punched in. They pretty much followed the fault lines Helen had pointed out (and sometimes marked with Magic Marker for a little work now or a lot more later, and had she ever been right about later!). You wouldn't even have noticed from the outside, but what remained on the inside was pretty much a Platonic conception—the *idea* of the interior of a house, to which the shadow of empirical reality had not been added. I began to grasp what real thoroughness must mean to the men in the Buick/Oldsmobile. I wondered if it was supposed to contain a message.

Before doing anything else I walked around to the backyard and paced off the distance to the spot where a line dropped at ninety degrees from the north tip of the empty goldfish pond bisected at another right angle a line from the diseased hawthorne tree. (Get it trimmed and sprayed, or you'll be paying to have it removed and replaced.) The ground where the tomato plants had been was hard, but not as hard as the lawn, and I hit the lockbox at about one and a half shovel depths. I was a little surprised that an excavating team had not beaten me to it.

With hourly flights out of LAX, I could assume that I had no more than a half-hour head start, but then I tend to have a hysterical personality. The fact that no Buick had been waiting two doors down told me that they were shorthanded, or that I was not such a high priority.

The box was a combination of 1960s paranoia (You have to be ready to go on a moment's notice! Where? I don't know, Europe, Kansas, Argentina) and the legacy of a family that had made some of its money in cash businesses. It contained four Krugerrands wrapped carefully between sheets of wax paper (purchased, alas, on the way down when they had seemed bargains at $650, now soon to be negotiable only if melted down for less than $300). It also contained the .38 Smith & Wesson that had come as a belated legacy from my Grampa Jack when Gran was moved into a home. I remembered the care with which he had cleaned and oiled it (I had no idea with what), and the rascally glee with which he had peppered away at redheaded woodpeckers who were doing so (relatively) little damage to the wood exterior of his attic gables, chasing survivors down the block until the police pulled over to explain the revolutionary changes in weapons ordinances that had come about since 1900.

It was a beautiful piece of machinery, cold and blue/black as are so few products any more in this plastic world. John Ruskin would have approved of it. It also held great sentimental value, but I had thought it best not to leave it around a house with a small child. There were two boxes of ammunition (one only half full) purchased around 1958. I assumed they would still fire. People still had a sense of craftsmanship in those days. I had no idea what to do with the Krugerrands.

The Buick had still not arrived when I pulled out. I drove into the Loop and left the car in the city underground, which seemed the cheapest alternative if I was eventually going to have to plead that I had lost the ticket. I called Laura Westin from the public phone by the ticket window and asked her to meet me at Berghoff.

"But I've had lunch and it's too early for dinner," she complained.

"Then we won't have to stand in line," I said.

"You really know how to get round a girl," she said.

I had always wondered how secretaries with union-scale salaries lived. Laura Westin's rooms were just far enough east to see the lake and walk to work but where she didn't have to pay a really serious status premium. It wasn't a pad, by any means, but at least her shelves had books and records and not that opaque and cloudy glassware that is owned by single women who sleep in hair nets. The furniture was a little Federalist for me, but you could tell that every item had been chosen with care.

I sat in the middle of a long Victorian cathouse sofa that was not as uncomfortable as it might have been and told her very nearly the whole story. I made careful distinctions between what I knew for a fact and what I suspected. She allowed me to narrate to the finish with only two or three witty interjections.

"Either you are telling me the truth as you know it," she said in measured voice," or you have altogether the most outrageous technique of seduction I have yet run into."

I had ended my story with a heavy hint about needing a place to lay up for a day or two. She seemed to be considering this. "You're welcome as long as you behave yourself. No eating outside the kitchen. And take off your shoes so you don't track mud on the carpets."

I promised heartily. "It's only a precaution in case they have the means for canvassing hotels. I could always camp out under the Hyde Park El, but I'm an indoor type. I much prefer to hide myself like the Naval Treaty."

She snickered, and I couldn't tell if she thought I was a paranoid schizophrenic or if she had missed the reference to Sherlock. "You think I'm being silly."

"Oh, no," she said. "And don't think I don't know my Conan Doyle. I was laughing about a story they told on my Aunt Sally when a friend of hers was taken to be examined at Bethesda Naval Hospital."

"Oh, yes?"

"She said, 'My goodness, these modern doctors *do* specialize.'"

She was so pleased with herself that she agreed to ring up Max.

We met for coffee at the Seminary Restaurant. Max didn't think much of the coffee.

"Ersatz," he said. "Hot water, they say in Europe. And what flavor there is, is just a little wrong. The whole modern world. Little substitutions, little departures from the real thing. Chemical approximations. Pretty soon the whole world we live in will be one giant forgery."

Max would have liked Grampa Jack's pistol, but he was going to have to settle for the satisfaction he got from his metaphor.

"Like the document?"

"I can tell you are looking for a yes or no answer. Thumbs up, thumbs down. It must be characteristically human to think only one's own insights may legitimately contain nuanced qualification and uncertainty."

"Okay," I said with resignation. "Give me the nuanced uncertainty, then."

"Let us consider the question of forgery," Max said. "It may be addressed through physical evidence, as in age and composition of paper and inks. In this case, of course, there being only a copy available, that is not possible to determine with precision."

I indicated agreement.

"So we must move to questions of content. In the first aspect, semiotics. The pure consistency of language. As I can work only with your translation, that must be left to you.

"In the second place, content of an objective nature. Dates, et cetera. Archaisms. Copies of the Magna Charta with reference to the Battle of Crécy, et cetera."

"Ha, ha," I said.

"Again, in this case, your area of expertise. In

fact, it is the least common error of forgers. Too easy to check."

"And?"

"That leaves what you might call the hermeneutical side. Subjective tone. The psychology of the author. The overall fittingness."

"Your area of expertise," I said.

"In a measure, yes," Max said. "But seldom for contemporary documents of this nature. I'm only a buff of the new stuff. Philological deconstruction of texts is either trendy crap or it's what rare-book people have been doing for centuries."

"Deconstruction?"

"A reading against the grain of surface content."

"And what does that have to do with forgery?" I said. "Give me a case."

"The Donation of Constantine," Max said instantly.

"A medieval manuscript?"

"It deeded the whole of Europe to the Church. Signed by the Emperor Constantine, his Last Will. A masterpiece of forgery. It was written by eighth-century monks and was believed for seven hundred years. The forgery was uncovered by a fifteenth-century Italian named Lorenzo Valla."

"Using semiotics or hermeneutics?"

"A little of both. Valla was a philologist. The Donation was written in eighth-century Latin The monks hadn't thought about that. But I think the thing that made Valla suspicious was something else. The document was just too perfect. It served the needs of the Church too well."

"What did deconstruction prove?"

"Not cotton-picking much if you were interested in Constantine," Max said. "But it ended up telling the world a lot about eighth-century monks."

"And our friend Latief?"

"Whether or not Latief was the author you'll have to work out for yourself. But parts of it strike me as sincere. The Donation was that way, too. The monks felt the world really *ought* to belong to the Church. The man who wrote your document had a strong sense of ambivalence. You can't make that kind of thing up. He is a man who lives at the border of two worlds, fully accepted by neither, an impostor, a full citizen of neither."

"That describes a double agent all right," I said.

"It does," Max said. "It also describes artists, immigrants, and schizophrenics. Not over half a million of the above within a five-mile radius. What else can I help you with?"

"Since you asked," I said. He knew already. I was paying for the coffee. "You could bring ecstatic happiness into my life if you were able to discover how the CIA handles its relationships with purveyors and proprietaries."

When I walked in, Laura Westin was sitting on the sofa playing with Grampa Jack's pistol. She was popping out the cartridge cylinder and popping it back in just the way I used to do as a child.

"I thought your shirts needed laundering," she said. I had left the pistol in my traveling bag. "You prove to be a man of unsuspected parts."

"My Grampa Jack's, and be careful with it."

"Oh, it's not loaded."

"Grampa Jack used to say there's no such thing as an unloaded gun, just a gun somebody thought was unloaded."

"And what did Grampa Jack do with it?"

"At the time I knew him he shot woodpeckers. Hit some of them, too."

"How about that!" Laura Westin said. "A wood-pecker-shooting peckerwood."

If there's one thing I can't stand, it's insults to my ancestry. "I'm surprised you know that term. I'm also afraid it's not polite. It may even be vulgar."

She gave the pistol a flick of the wrist, snapping the cylinder into place. It's a trick I had tried to do for years, but I could never get the knack of it.

"It's a big one," she said.

"It's a standard thirty-eight. It'll make a pretty good hole, though."

"In a woodpecker?"

"It's been an arduous day," I said. "If you'll just spare me a pillow and an old blanket, I'll sleep on the sofa."

"You'll do no such thing," she said.

She was gone about forty seconds, and what she had when she returned was not a blanket but two glasses and a bottle of Glenlivet. "Now drink this." Her voice did not admit of discussion. "It will calm your nerves."

She took half of her own in a single swallow and didn't cough or make a face. She put down the glass and started to unbutton the front of her starchy white blouse. "Now don't avert your eyes, but don't stare and make some peculiar thing out of this either."

In the morning I woke to the smell of bacon and eggs cooking. It hadn't taken me long to admit to an iota or two of curiosity about Westin's petite breasts. They were really quite fine, and so were her legs. I had no previous experience of older women except for a vulgar schoolboy rhyme. Grampa Jack had always extolled their virtues, but I had always thought that was just a polite little minuet he did for Gran. Westin had energy, though. In fact, she was great. Before rolling toward my shoes, I checked my body part by part. Except for carpet burns on the knees, the injuries were all internal. I was trying to put together exactly the right kind of compliment to greet her with at breakfast. I wanted to be considerate. I didn't want her to have to be Grateful. I was still working on it as she dished up the scrambled eggs.

"You were quite a surprise; here, have some bacon," she said. "No, take another piece; don't be bashful. Now who ever would have thought a dry old stick like Keith McCallum had that in him?"

She was Grateful all right.

20.
Geologist

Sex is well and good, but in the final analysis it doesn't *solve* anything. When I was finished with the scrambled eggs, I had to face the fact that I was on the run. There was no other way of looking at it. My house was a shambles, and there was just no way of sleeping in it without a day or two of work by an electrical contractor. They were probably just wait ing for me to come back to give me one of those funny heart attacks. It made me do some serious tactical thinking. When you can't go back, the only thing left is to go forward. Something I was doing was bothering somebody. I didn't know how to stop bothering them. All I could do was try to bother them a whole lot more. I was going to go on doing what I was doing, only more so. It was a way of going over to the attack. It didn't take Westin long to work out that Socony-

Vacuum was a subsidiary of the old Socony-Mobil, which they now called Mobil Oil.

The people at Mobil live in a world with a high level of trust. It is a pretty fundamental business, without any secrets to steal, and the last time they tried a tender offer it turned out to be Monkey Ward. None of the people I talked to had ever heard of my work on Indonesian oil policy, but none of them doubted that I was putting together background data for an article on the Tokyo Agreements. And I was, I was. The name of the Socony-Vacuum head man in Palembang in 1965 was Hal Leitsey, and the fourth person I talked to was able to produce his retirement address and telephone number in Connecticut. His tour had been from 1963 to 1967.

I gave Leitsey the same story. I could probably have passed a polygraph on it. Since I was flying east anyway (the poly might have done a slight zig), he would see me the following morning. Westin was at work, so I made my own reservations. I was trying to work out the elaborate piece of fiction I was going to have to write for the SEAAAC auditors.

I rented an Avis at LaGuardia and set out north on 684 picking up 7 out of Danbury all the way to Cornwall. What kind of geek spent his life traveling all over the world in order to retire in Connecticut? I was about to find out. I found Leitsey's house after only two sets of right-at-the-split-oak-left-at-the-red-barn directions. It looked like it might have a plaque marking it as the site where English settlers first discovered succotash.

Leitsey met me on the porch steps the way frontier settlers meet people to decide if they can be let in the house. He was tall, late sixtyish, and balding, but he had the kind of muscles you can get only from working with pipes and valves. He had an American business face, with the smooth edges roughed off, and I would have bet a hundred bucks that within five minutes he would show me a tool or a gadget. I would have won, too. The price of entrance was examination of the antique lock that secured the front door, and the tools with which he had repaired it. There was a brief excursus on the wood pegs that held together the beams.

"Our retirement project," he said. "When we're done, every object in the house, every fixture, every repair, will be authentic 1700. Doing the work myself. Dumb hobby, eh?"

I didn't think it was any dumber than about ten thousand others. I mumbled something polite. Snapshots of Leitseys, Dad, Mom, two boys, one girl, were displayed on mantels and shelf surfaces, usually with an elephant or a camel in the background. America itself was an unknown. America was Romance.

"What I'd like to hear about first," I said "is your memories of Supervision."*

In the beginning it had been the small stuff. They stopped you at customs for a going-over. They asked your children whether they believed in one God. Then they pulled visas. Pretty soon he was running a little short on trained engineers.

---

*A policy proposed by Aidit and the PKI and approved by Sukarno under which government and labor-union officials "supervised" oil-company managements.

Leitsey had a kind of studied value neutrality. There was nothing personal or ideological to it. Communists were like mosquitos or crocodiles. They were doing what their species did. They were simply a factor that set back his lifting schedule.

Supervision made things serious. The radicals must have gotten the upper hand in Jakarta. Colonel Sutomo had taken to bicycling over after dark to warn him when there were demonstrations. Sometimes he parked an armored car in front of the American compound just to be sure. But just to give you the tenor of the times, Sutomo had requisitioned Leitsey's private jeep.

"I told him to go to hell," Leitsey said. "I told him I wasn't authorized. It was the property of Vacuum Oil."

"When was the crisis?"

"Oh, in retrospect, it was that spring. By then we were down to about ten people from a hundred and thirty. They were getting a little crazy I began to worry that the Commies might think the best trick for getting their way was to create an incident. A half dozen or so dead Americans."

"You had a heavy responsibility," I said.

"I mean," he said. "Governments don't understand that kind of thing. They don't have a bottom line. They just pull their people. Socony-Vacuum has stockholders. You have to look at costs. Dependent transportation for a place like Palembang is not trivial. Leaves and length of tour were strictly controlled."

"So it was your decision whether to stay or cut and run?"

"Manila didn't want to deal with it. I was the man on site. Lives or dollars? You probably think it's crass. I wasn't sleeping well. But one thing you learn in business, there is always an acceptable level of risk."

I could relate to the part about sleeping. "You knew Francis Cole at that time?"

He gave me a look. "The embassy wasn't being very helpful. They didn't care much about problems up in Sumatra. Things like drilling technique. It wasn't easy in Indo. You get ten thousand tons a well-year against a hundred and fifty thousand in Kuwait. And quality differential. Indo oil is sweet, which means it isn't loaded down with sulfur, but it has a lot of paraffin. To get it down from Lirik we had to steam-heat the pipeline to forty degrees Celsius and use special tankers. Try explaining that to an economics officer."

"Francis Cole understood about paraffinic oil?"

"Frank understood the business point of view. He worked for AID, but he wasn't a dufus like the embassy people. He also had some good native sources."

"I imagine that made him a pretty good adviser," I said. "I'll bet he said stay."

"He said stick it out at least until September," Leitsey acknowledged. "He warned that things might appear to get worse before they got better. He understood businessmen's risks."

"So you stayed."

"Corporate HQ panicked and pulled the plug. Dependents were rotated. The funny thing was that they weren't actually moved until December, when the crisis was really over. I always recommended sticking. It gave me quite a reputation at the home office."

"And some hairy moments, I bet."

"Oh, the month after the coup we found these big holes in the woods. Sutomo said they were deer traps. One day the soldiers came to the wax plant and asked for bags. They took our whole inventory. Bodies started floating up to the mouth of the river and we had to keep the women and children indoors. I asked Sutomo to dump them farther out."

"It was pretty sharp of Cole to pinpoint September, didn't you think?"

Leitsey turned his head and gave me a long look out of the corner of his eye. "Now, everybody knew Frank Cole was some kind of spook. That was obvious. He was a little too sharp to be counting rice sacks. I mean, assignment to the lateral programs is usually reserved to junior FSOs who eat the maharaja's wife's salad. Young goofs from Harvard and middle-aged screwups who use the wrong spoon for soup. That item about the PKI distributing American grain—Frank Cole would have rolled that up in a long weekend. Maybe he did. Anyway, he and his pal Bill Allbright had gotten themselves quite a reputation up in Sumatra. I mean, they were legends. Hey, listen, you didn't come up here just to talk about the Tokyo Agreements, did you?"

"Not entirely," I confessed. I told him he was very astute.

His Marge came out with American coffee and homemade cheesecake. She really was the woman who canvassed my house for the local Republicans.

I thought she could deal with bodies in wax bags if she had to. She stayed just long enough to inform me that one son was with Honeywell Greece and the other with Citibank Manila. Their daughter was a senior at Yale and was spending the summer on an archeological dig in Cameroon. "Now I'll leave you men to talk business."

"I'm just thinking," I said. "I'm thinking Frank Cole must have asked some kind of quid pro quo for that kind of information. There must have been something you could do for him in return."

Leitsey gave me one more sideways look. "You're not a radical journalist, are you?"

"I'm not a journalist," I assured him. "You can call my dean or look me up in a biography book."

He looked mollified. "He did ask a favor once."

"Up in Sumatra."

"The mail to Sumatra was unreliable," he said. It was said apologetically. It had probably once been his cover story if he got caught. "He asked me to carry some letters in a pouch."

"For Colonel Sutomo?"

"No. Or at least not at first. They were for some colonel on General Mokoginta's staff. But Sutomo met my flight because the other colonel's flight was delayed out of Medan. Sutomo made them hold the plane. He took a quick look and gave the pouch to the other colonel who was waiting in a jeep." He seemed relieved, as if he had gotten a guilty secret off his chest.

"And you did this for three years?"

"Like holy hell! I did it once. That plane-holding stuff made me realize what kind of mess it could be.

I told Frank I worked for Socony-Mobil. I'm a company man. I couldn't risk a seventy-million-dollar investment over some kind of CIA hanky-panky. I told him to get himself another boy."

"So what did Frank do?"

"Just what I said. He got another boy."

"Who?" I said. "Whom, I mean. Did he get?"

"Marlon," Leitsey said.

"Marlon?"

"Marlon Crockett. Don't be dense. He was the chief geologist at Caltex. Couldn't find liquid with a dowsing stick, either. It goes to show."

It was a nervous drive back down 7. All the way I kept trying to tell myself how clever I had been to get all that out of Leitsey. But if I was so clever, why wasn't I happy? At least there wasn't a persistent dented Buick or Oldsmobile in my rearview mirror. If anybody was following me, as they say in the spook books, they were awfully good. The thought failed to cheer me up. What cheered me up was my long-distance call to Westin. She had gotten the Tech Systems reports. Crockett and Oren Lewes had both been on the board for the past two years. The year before that it had been Crockett and one Francis S. K. Cole. It was a mandala, if only you knew what it meant. To understand it, I was going to have to renew acquaintance with an old friend. I went to work rearranging my plane tickets. It's hard when there's a break in the relationship, but sometimes you just have to force yourself.

21.
Teddy's

Now this interview was going to have to be handled exactly right. Teddy's Rough Rider lounge is located in Tyson Corner, Virginia. There isn't any Teddy. There are damn few Rough Riders, either. Actually, it's a Ramada Inn. They are strictly an equal-access innkeeper, and they let in just about anybody who pays and behaves himself, including the day shift from Langley.

I backed my Avis into the parking stall. Grampa Jack believed in doing all the little nuisance details first, and also eating your peas before dessert. It was the kind of little touch that doesn't matter ninety-nine times out of a hundred, but that hundredth it matters a lot.

There was a general air of free conviviality. Three beefcakes with Beefeaters were sitting at a table with a thin professorial type in tweed coat who from the way he commanded the table must have been at least a GS-18. He was holding forth loudly about something that made all three of them angry. I wasn't able to tell out of context whether it was Russians or Democratic congressmen. Nobody was bothering to whisper, or even talk softly. For all I knew, every other table might contain three Vladimirs, but somebody apparently knew better. I had heard they sent tech boys over once or twice a week to do an electronic sweep.

Three men were sitting at the end of the bar, holding one of those animated discussions in which the man on the middle stool is constantly in danger of going over the side and getting a nasty bump on the back of the head. It might have had something to do with Nicaragua. "It's a simple matter of peeling potatoes," the nearer one was saying. "When I was nine my parents sent me off to Boy Scout camp, where you had to pull a tour in the kitchen. These were Boy Scouts, mind, and I tried peeling the potatoes the way it says in the manual, with the knife pointed away from your hand. I peeled about four potatoes in half an hour. The cook gave me an awful ass-chewing. Then this old nigger who worked in the kitchen came out to help me. He showed me how you really peel potatoes, with the blade curled back toward your hand. It worked okay, but I told him about the technique in the Scout manual. 'Listen, son,' he says. 'The stuff they says in them manuals is just for if you cuts yourself. But don't kid yourself, boy, they doesn't care how you does it. They wants them potatoes peeled.'"

He was the beefcake of the triad. I had managed

to mosey up behind the professorial one, whose turn it now was to hold forth. "The covert side is like the unconscious," he was saying. "You can think of it in Freudian terms, if you like. The ego, superego, and id. The superego, the part that has all the small child's priggishness, doesn't want to know. *We* are the things that happen in the night. *We* are the stuff out of their nightmares. They like it that way, because the things we do have deniability for the daytime person. They try not to see too clearly. It's called blockage. The problem comes not when we do something especially outrageous but when we slip and do something they can't avoid seeing. Then the shit hits the fan. The id and the superego get mixed up, and the superego is compelled to rise up and start making rules and restrictions. Sin and revivalism, schizophrenia, it's the oldest national character trait. It doesn't mean they want to kill off the id, it just means the superego wants to live behind a cordon sanitaire." The beefy guy was nodding hard. I took one more step and brought myself into the prof's peripheral vision.

"Hello, Oren," I said. I gave him a friendly pop on the back. "Long time."

"Keith," he echoed weakly. "It's been years."

"Not since the Malaysian tin project," I prodded.

"Has it been that long? Say, I'm still sorry about the way that turned out."

"No hard feelings, pal, I've long since forgotten it." I was quite sincere. I truly was. "Say, though, you could do something for me if you remember. I was trying to look up an old boy named Bill Allbright. I need to talk to him about one of my projects."

"Bill Allbright." Oren seemed to be pondering this new and unexpected name. "To tell the truth, I've sort of lost contact with him. I suppose I could look him up in the files. How about tomorrow?"

"Oh, come on, Oren," said the Potato Peeler. "You guys at IG must still have Allbright by the short hairs for flying illegal cargoes all over the Pacific Rim. The crazy son of a bitch. Didn't you pull his passport and ship him out to Frisco to run the proprietary air, what is it, Pacair or something like that?"

Oren Lewes was white as a sheet.

"Well, how about that?" I said. "My wife and kid live out there, with her new husband. Maybe I'll get a chance to drop in on Bill."

I gave Oren another clap on the back and shook hands with the two Potato Peelers. "So long, pal," I said. It was like snipping a lock from King Saul's beard. I walked out of Teddy's at just the right speed. The car started on the first pump, which not all Avises do, you know, and I moved with what the Supreme Court likes to call deliberate speed out of the lot, onto the street, and onto the expressway that would take me to Dulles. There was every probability that Oren was still squirming in his chair and pontificating to the two Operations men, but I played the percentages.

There was space on the first flight to San Francisco. In artillery spotting it is called bracketing. You fire a round way over the target, then you fire a round way under. You do the same thing left and right. Each time you drop or add a little less until you just know your next round is going to be a hit. It sounds expensive in terms of ammunition, and it is, just like it was going to be expensive for the SEAAAC travel account. It's worth it, though. It gets you right on the button when you finally say FFE* and drop however many tons of WP or HE† ordnance on whoever is the poor intended target.

---

*Fire For Effect
†WP: White Phosphorus; HE: High Explosive

22.
Potato Peeler

I was up and down about calling Helen when I arrived. It would be nice to spend a couple of hours with Jeremy, but the custody agreement had been specific about this sort of popping in. I have always tended to take the English view of contractual obligations. A rule is a rule, and a deal is a deal. Helen, on the other hand, tends to take the Russian view. A deal is a deal as long the circumstances that prompted you to make it remain in force. If she had been in my shoes, she wouldn't have hesitated for an instant. It's the old poly-sci problem of how the good and honest folks of the world should cope with those who are less so.

I compromised. I watched Jeremy across the schoolyard for about ten minutes before he saw me and came running over. He acted as if this sort of meeting was absolutely the normal thing. Keeping secrets from his mother and Lieberman was going to be good training for life. I mentioned the kris, and we agreed the way to get it past Lieberman was to send it to a school friend who had wayward and irresponsible parents. He wrote out the friend's address on the back of one of my American Express receipts. I could tell the whole idea appealed to him a lot.

"In Indonesia and Malaya it's not only a weapon," I told him. "The warriors used to think that it contained their souls. Anthropologists would probably say that the symbolic importance is a function of the scarcity of toolmaking metals and the importance of a personal weapon in that society."

"Did you use it in a fight?" Jeremy wanted to know.

"Nope," I said. "And you'd better not either. In fact, you better hide it for a while. If Mom discovers it, you just say you've had it for years."

"That's pretty smart, Dad." He was easily impressed. "You know everything, Dad."

"Not quite," I said modestly.

Allbright's office was another one of those warehouse places, this time on the fringe of San Francisco International, but for some reason he had taken the afternoon off. I managed to get the secretary to reveal where he lived without quite realizing that she had. It was a layered ranch house in the Japano–Frank Lloyd Wright tradition looking down from the Marin hills toward Alcatraz. I might have wondered how he paid for it on government salary without becoming a candidate for Alcatraz himself, but I had stopped wondering about those things. Sometimes a properly placed man on a short leash can still do very well for himself.

I thought I would just ring the bell and surprise him, but he wasn't all that surprised. He had the cheerful you-got-me manner of the unrepentant white-collar criminal. He was a man who knew what he wanted in life, and a house on a hill in Marin County was part of it. Going for it had just been a part of life, and so had getting caught. The other thing he had wanted passed me on the way out dressed in a rather severe business suit with a small valise in her hand. She gave Allbright a proprietary peck on the cheek and a nice squeeze of the hand.

"Stew with Singapore Air," he said as she disappeared. "You probably think, look at that old fool! She's away half the time getting boffed by Australian grain brokers and Jappo computer salesman. You know what I think, though? Deep down, out of the suspicions bred by years in the trade, I seriously doubt it. None like an old one, huh? You know why? Who would she ever find as interesting as me? Not some Jap steel salesman, that's for sure. What do you think? No, don't say. You've got to have trust, that's the thing they say these days."

He paused to knock on the ornate teak chest.

"Thought I might bring her into the outfit in a year or two when S.A. takes her off flight duty. Run a security check, everything. Easy enough, though you have to have time to run down the Chinese connections. Cousins. Serve for the marrying papers too."

He didn't even ask, he was making me a straight gin, which he advertised as the Allbright Sling.

"You can call Oren Lewes to check my bona fides," I said.

"Fuck Oren," he said.

"Then tell me about Frank Cole."

"It's a sad thing," Allbright said. "People who don't approve of Frank should remember how he picked up his bad habits."

It was sad, all right. Frank Cole and Bill Allbright had first met at FE-5 in the 1950s. Cole had been a step or two farther along, and it had stayed that way. They had worked together about half the time.

"You have to understand what it was like in the fifties," he went on. "Kim Roosevelt, the Dulleses, Lansdale. Not a bunch of half-assed professors and computer jockeys. Half of them came from families that had had ten mil net worth in 1900. They were out of the money business entirely and into the hobby of running the world."

"Frank was born to money?"

"That's a good one. The name on his birth certificate was Kohl, K-O-H-L. As in lumpendeutsch for cabbage. He changed it while he was in college, when he was being checked out for the OSS. He had already gotten the picture."

"And was accepted as one of the boys?"

"He sat there in the office while Dulles and Roosevelt created the modern world. Drew lines on a map and said that's how it would be. He was a fully paid-up, card-carrying member. One of the Great Old Ones. Present at the Creation. With Angleton in Italy, K.R. in Tehran, and Lansdale on the Magsaysay and Diem capers. Frank carried the suitcases. All that's finished now. The computer boys and the deep thinkers have taken over. Frank was the last of his breed. The last of the great swashbucklers. The last of the Cold War cowboys."

"And his downfall was money."

"The lack of money," Allbright corrected, "is the root of all evil. When you've walked through airports with suitcases that have millions, when you've created Presidents and Shahanshahs, you don't just retire on a pension to a housing project on the West Coast of Florida."

I was touched by Allbright's sociological explanation of crime. It no doubt explained his own willingness to carry illegal cargoes all over Asia.

"He was my mentor," Allbright mused. "He was the best friend I ever had."

"Tell me about Sumatra in 1958," I said.

"Oh, yes, that. Terrific operation, Sumatra. To understand Sumatra, you start with a map. It was a simple matter of gerrymandering. We had worked it out that we couldn't do much with Sukarno, so we simply drew a line around everything we wanted in the area, and at that time it was mainly Sumatra. Then we persuaded half a dozen young colonels that they could take it for themselves and live off the fat of the land."

"It didn't work."

"Did it ever not! It was one of those really terrible ideas that look great on paper. Sumatra had a population that looked like it might vote the right way in the Cold War. Some deep thinkers in the DDA thought the military in Jakarta might split down the middle. What actually happened, Nasution went in with a few battalions of paratroops and ran our asses off to Sulawesi inside two months. Uneffingmitigated fiasco. The ambassador in Jakarta broke his lying machine trying to explain our role in it."

"Did Sumatra contribute to Frank Cole's inferiority complex?"

"Frank was a good soldier," Allbright snapped. "He didn't approve, but he did his job."

"Didn't approve why?"

"Frank always said you never mess with a person. You leave him alone, or you kill him fricking dead. Sumatra was messing with. There were too many places for it to bugger up, and even if you won you hadn't accomplished anything. Try telling that kind of thing to Allen Dulles. Frank was in a bit of a sulk about it. Had him a hell of a pretty woman, though. One Dalippah from Medan, working out of Jakarta, an army C.E. That was the best stunt he pulled off in Sumatra."

"What stunt?"

"Treason never doth prosper. Frank saw the handwriting and managed to get her out of there. Packed her off to Jakarta and even managed to wangle her a job on the staff back there. She would bat it out from Jakarta every few weeks to shack with Frank. For a guerrilla soldier with a radio and a handful of rice, that's good living."

"I'm not sure I understand," I said. "I thought the colonels in Medan were rebels and the army in Jakarta stayed loyalist."

"You got it exactly," Allbright said. "That's the stunt all right. Frank used his private old-boy network. I think he even bounced some messages through FE-5 and the embassy. He must have had some kind of chips to call in in Jakarta. All those guys were cousins, anyway. It's not a bad trick, when you think about it. Like a Confederate adviser getting his girlfriend off the staff of General Lee and shipping her up to work for General Grant."

"And arranging for conjugal visits."

"Civil war is a fluid situation. This one more than most."

"Did it cross your mind that his friends in Jakarta might have ulterior motives? That Dalippah was part of a horse trade. Frank didn't believe in the operation anyway."

"Now, now, sir. Frank was a good soldier, as I said. I think you're suggesting that he did a very naughty thing. Our job was to run a small civil war, and we ran it. Never mind that we had an ambassador in Jakarta with his nose four inches up Sukarno's wazoo."

"Where is Cole now?"

Allbright gave me a long sly look. There was something important about Cole I still didn't get, and Allbright wasn't going to be any help. That's why he hadn't felt it necessary to call Oren. Oren had called him.

I let it drop. I wasn't even quite sure why he had told me as much as he had, unless he got carried away in the pure exuberance of it. He had helped me more than he could possibly know. I knew, for instance, who the girl was in the portrait on Moko's wall. Cole had had a way with women, all right, and he hadn't been bashful about putting it to use. I had a pretty good idea how Sukarno had been persuaded to believe in a coup by his military staff.

There were no brick-eating gorillas in the queue at the gate, I made sure of that, but they appeared just as I was done tucking my carry-on bag under the seat. I was already buckled up. I was seat 24A, and they were 24B and 24C, which shows how small a world it was becoming. They had done a pretty good job of waiting until the last minute, because I could hear all sort of hydraulic doors in the process of closing. I didn't even try to look surprised.

What I did was give them my version of All-bright's you-got-me expression. Then I waited a few seconds until the baggage van's withdrawal was visible out of the corner of my eye. I had already quietly unbuckled, just as the sign suggested I do the opposite. I bolted up so quickly that nothing could have stopped me without a public ruckus. I was yelling "I'm sick" loud enough that the stewardess couldn't ignore me and was all too happy to hold the ramp thirty seconds to get me off her airplane. I was happy that United wasn't the only airline flying between San Francisco and the Middle West. I was also happy that I had taken the precaution of double booking, even if the airline companies frown on it. Just to be sure, I hadn't made the second reservation in my own name. It took me most of the time before the flight, which was to Milwaukee, to straighten out the ticket and save SEAAAC a buck.

It wasn't exactly a relaxing flight. There was a little burst of turbulence, and I was starting to worry about all sorts of things. Life, death, meaning, infinity. I worried about my friends, and whether they really were. All the little irritants that occupy paranoiacs in the idle moments when they are not actively trying to find out what people are saying about them behind their backs.

If I included Laura Westin in my worries, I needn't have bothered. She was waiting up on the sofa with her legs tucked under her and a historical romance in her hands. It was one of those books with a pirate and a woman in a negligee on the cover. Westin was wearing pretty much the same negligee and it looked like it might be brand-new.

"No rest for the weary," she said.

23.
Charts

Sorel was okay too. He met me at the Bull and Bear with a folder full of stock price and volume charts. He spread them out on the place mat where the waitress was hoping to put a five-dollar hamburger and a three-dollar Bloody Mary. Sorel asked for two coffees. She gave him a dirty look, and he told her to go ahead and make the coffees Irish.

The charts he was most interested in looked like this:

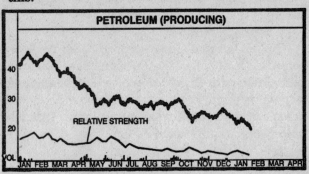

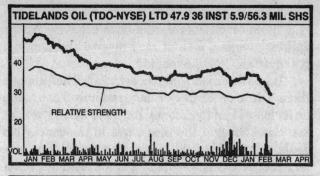

TIDELANDS OIL (TDO-NYSE) LTD 47.9 36 INST 5.9/56.3 MIL SHS

RELATIVE STRENGTH

INDOIL (IOL-NYSE) LTD 251.7 49 INST 11.1/44.7 MIL SHS

RELATIVE STRENGTH

Sorel was a great believer in them, but I had to be convinced. "I don't understand," I said. "Don't you want to know things like whether the company is making any money?"

"Doesn't matter," Sorel insisted. "It's already in the price. That's all you need to watch."

"How does it work?"

"When a stock moves up on volume, you know somebody is accumulating. Whoever it is, he knows something you don't. When it moves down on volume, he's bailing out. You watch for volume on key reversals, and you don't worry about moves that take place when trading is dull."

"But *why* does it work?"

"Because charts record human behavior. At the darkest moment, a chart may reverse and turn up. It's mystical. It's like magic."

It was an encouraging thought. Indoil had jumped three points on Friday on megavolume. That made up its losses and then some. It hit the *WSJ* new high list. Sorel thought the secret was in the chart. "No doubt about it," he said. "A classic accumulation pattern. Big Friday moves coming in the last hour when everybody is lulled to sleep."

"How long has this been going on?" I asked.

"Oh, since last September at the very least. Before that, you might get away with calling the formation a base. You'll see relative strength start to pick up in August. Then in September the beginning of higher peaks and valleys, more volume. The breakout."

"Tell me honestly you were never a spook," I said.

"I was in the army before Vietnam really heated up," Sorel said. "I worked in the motor pool at Fort Hood. Got clap twice and made Speck Five in two years. Straight AUS."

The waitress arrived with our Irish coffees and stole a quick glance over Sorel's shoulder. "Will there be anything else?" she wondered. She wrote out the check while keeping a casual focus on the charts. I wondered if this week's tips were going into Indoil.

"Want a tip?" Sorel asked.

She gave a big smile.

"Then buzz off," Sorel said. It took fifteen seconds for the smile to do a slow transformation into a sulk. Puns weren't her thing.

"Let me be sure I have this straight," I said. "Tidelands has been falling steadily because the whole oil industry is in trouble."

"Check," Sorel said. "With little spikes whenever there were rumors of a buyout. Amateurs to the slaughter. We sold short when your Mrs. Westin called our attention to one of those spikes."

"While Indoil has been going up against the trend."

"Check again," Sorel said.

"And it has been going up since last September." I didn't mind appearing to be a little slow. "Which means that whatever big boy is buying started buying then."

"You're hitting homers on every pitch," Sorel said.

"Could it have been anybody other than Crockett?"

"This is a stock chart, boy, not a crystal ball. You want that kind of info, you hire yourself an industrial snoop. But based on what you know and what happened today, there are pretty good odds it was Crockett's people."

"How could he avoid the reporting requirements?"

"Lots of ways," Sorel said. "Lots of little partners. Friendly risk arbs. A tacit agreement rather than a legal one."

"I guess we'll just have to wait and see."

"Like hell," Sorel said. "It was on the ticker this

morning. Crockett filed with the SEC yesterday. This morning he announced the terms of his tender offer. Indoil is halted, of course, with indications of up about seven points. Tidelands is off three on the news."

"Whoopee!" I said. I had never made a killing before on anything. "Better call Laura Westin and tell her it's time to cover."

"Already done," Sorel said. "I called before I left the office, but she beat me to it. She covered when the news came over FNN."

I thought about it on the way over to Max's apartment. Maybe I was at the low point on the chart where things started to turn up. What it felt more like, though, was circles. I was running in them. One of them contained Moko and Siti and Dalippah. Another one contained an ex-spook named Frank Cole, a current spook named Oren Lewes, and an oil man named Marlon Crockett. The only thing the two circles had in common was a little dot in the center. I was that dot.

I once had a student who believed that the university wasn't real. He thought that when he got off the El a little man on the twenty-eighth floor of UH said, "All right, wind it up, here he comes." My life was starting to feel like that. Marlon Crockett had sent me off to Indonesia to negotiate a deal that he had, in fact, already started to make. Now why had he done that? And if there was a plausible explanation, why did he lie about it? While I was in Indonesia I had been given a document explaining the 1965 coup, about which I had written a paper in grad school, published a month before my trip. Everything seemed to be happening in reverse order. It was what Max would have called a deconstruction. The causes of things were getting upside down and ass backwards. Max would have said that it merely lacked closure, the part of a story that ties up the loose ends and imparts that satisfying feeling of completeness. He claimed that it was a literary conceit, and they stopped putting it into books when they realized it didn't exist in real life. About 41 percent of everything, Max said, remains unexplained.

I tried to think in an orderly fashion. I had learned of Cole as a result of the Latief confession. I had received the Latief confession while in Indonesia for Crockett. But Crockett had gone ahead with Indoil as if my negotiations were redundant. Then what were Moko and I talking about? Then there was the heart-attack rate, which was suddenly way up among old friends of mine and even people who merely spoke to me on the telephone. I was weighed down with problems old and new. Maybe this was the low point. One of the new little nags was Max. He had called in sick at the library, and whoever answered his phone wanted to receive information rather than give it, to wit: my name.

Max's apartment was only four blocks from the El station, but it was on one of those funny little streets that try to make you believe Chicago is not laid out like a waffle iron. It occupied a floor in one of those brownstone townhouses where the difference between luxury and a slum is the percentage of windows that contain flowerboxes. It's one of those streets where you can't find a parking place any time of day or night on either side of the street, legal or illegal, even though 90 percent of the cars are little foreign jobs, and try getting in there with a police ambulance, three squads, and two local news vans.

The neighbors didn't like it, they loved it and came out in mass to enjoy. You'd be surprised how many affluent urban brownstone types don't go to work during the day, or else work at home. By the time I worked my way into the circle, they were coming out with the body, and I could recognize Max even with a sheet over his head. I hardly even needed to check the Italian shoes. I just knew.

"No, there are no unusual aspects that I am at liberty to discuss at this time," the lieutenant was telling the blonde from Channel 5. "There were certain peculiarities, yes. Last year there were eight hundred and ninety-one murders in the city of Chicago. You learn in criminology that out of that many events, you are going to have a few that are abnormal."

While he was talking, I picked out the Buick. I was pretty sure they had picked me out too. They were doing their best to persuade the cop directing traffic to let them be the last car through. He was being a hardhead about it. The ambulance was ready to move out, and they were going to have to back out as soon as the cars behind them got the word and circle the block. The two heavies were discussing furiously. The driver seemed to want the other one to get out and go after me.

It wasn't the moment for running. It was going to be one of those odd races like egg and spoon, or the diddletwit Olympic walk, which are not always to the swift. I'm not much of a runner, but I can walk as fast as anybody, and I had a head start. By the end of the block Crewcut still wasn't in sight, and it was one of those corners where you have three options. I chose the middle one, and just to be sure, I ducked inside STANKUS REALTY and spent forty-five minutes looking into the possibility of investing in some near-north real estate. The agent and I were discussing fifteen- versus twenty-five-year mortgages when Crewcut walked by. I didn't leave until twenty minutes after he had passed again going the other way. "Hey, thanks," I told Mr. Stankus, "and I'll call you right away when I'm ready to take the plunge."

When I sat down on the El my hands started to shake. Max was dead. It was more than the loss of a friend. It was like losing a—resource. It was going to be as if you woke up one morning and they had taken away the Louvre, or the Uffizi. You couldn't get round it all at once. It was the sort of thing that would keep coming at you in little flashes for the rest of your life. I began running down the list of people I knew or had talked to. I wondered if I ought to call Leitsey or Allbright. Sorel, I thought, could look after himself, but I needed to catch up with Laura Westin. I was becoming an unhealthy person to know, talk to, or do business with. A regular Typhoid Mary.

I decided to go to my office first. I would just run in and catch Westin before closing, tell her I was making other arrangements, and have her check into a motel for a couple of nights. I wasn't sure whether to tell her about Max. There was a delay at Lake

Transfer, of course, and I missed her by five minutes. The reception secretary was just closing the mail room, and she insisted I take my mail.

There was an overdue notice to Gilmore's *World of Humanism* buried in the middle of it, which was the agreed-upon device if Max suddenly decided he believed in my paranoia. I was going to have to find time later to mourn. First I had a task to do. I would call Laura from one of the library phones.

It's haste, of course, that always puts the goose in the skillet. Grampa Jack always said do one thing at a time, correctly, don't be stewing the rabbit while you try to hold the rifle steady.

Now a Renaissance scholar wouldn't have had to use the card catalog, but what can you do? It just wasn't my specialty. I had to look up the call number, no apologies necessary, and that turned out to be my downfall. Max's office is just down the center aisle, and that had to be the point where they picked me up.

The Gilmore book was on 4 North. I wasn't familiar with the area at all. I trailed along the shelf ends looking at all the PWs and trying to get to the PZs. I couldn't believe there were so many PWs. That's the way it is when you wander into an unrelated field. I thought about all they had recently discovered about that part of the Middle Ages. And to think in my day it was just the Magna Charta and the improved horse collar.

The section of PZs I needed was off in one of those dark little alcoves that are set into the wall like private chapels in medieval churches. It was faster to try to go by subject headings. I wanted to get quickly from original sources to scholarly commentaries. I ran quickly past Dante and Marsilio Ficino. In the gap somebody had left between Pico della Mirandola and Aeneas Silvius Piccolomini (Pope Pius II), I saw the upper half of a crewcut head.

I tiptoed right on past the Gilmore and picked out Runciman's *Sicilian Vespers* before bolting toward the checkout desk with a firm Olympic walk. There was no sign of anyone in pursuit. The street was deserted too, except for the man fixing the flat on a Fiat.

I remembered that I still hadn't called Westin, and I was feeling so bad about it that I didn't recognize the tire changer until the other one was right on top of me. He had his hand in his overcoat pocket. The tire fixer straightened up with the tire tool in his hand.

"Okay," I said. "You got me."

What else was there to say?

"Let's go," said Hands-in-Pocket, aka my old friend Princeton.

Even though I had rehearsed how to run for it during a hundred gangster movies, I bent to get into the backseat.

"Not there," Princeton said.

I was just about to say something clever about the front seat being cramped and uncomfortable, and dangerous too, when a shove sent me stumbling along the side of the car and something dull but solid thudded down on my medulla oblongata. My eyes were open long enough to see the yawning mouth of the open car trunk. My mouth worked long enough to say the airline-pilot prayer. "Shit."

24.
Claustrophobia

It was hard to be really sure whether I was awake because of the dark. I didn't care for it much. The dark usually doesn't bother me, but this dark had real texture. It was sort of numb behind my right ear, which was another thing I didn't like. I had a bad feeling it was just the advance skirmish line of terrific pain.

Also there was a dull ache in the middle of my back where something had come down on it hard like a car trunk. Then I remembered. A car trunk had come down on it. Unless something really nice had happened in my sleep, that was where I still was. I gave my arm a little jerk and felt a sharp implement jab into my side. It was cold and rough like the edge of a jack.

A sort of electric shock wave started in my chest and ran down to my feet and up again to my head in slow motion. It was an adrenaline tide. I held my breath and started to count to ten. I had gotten to eight when all hell broke loose. There was some kind of wild animal in the trunk thrashing around in every direction at once. It was me. It was I. My arms and legs were pumping as hard as they could in every direction. Except that they didn't move. I was wedged tight.

The next thing the wild animal did was to give its sex-in-extremis scream. It reached far back in its throat for a guttural growl that would rise into a piercing shriek. Except there wasn't any sound. My body wasn't the only thing that was wedged tight. They had stuffed a ball of cloth in my mouth and bound it in with a gag. Now when had they found the time to do that? The thought of it made me want to scream again, which did nothing but jam a flap of cloth against the back of my throat. I couldn't breathe.

If this wasn't the low point on the chart, we were getting pretty close. There was so much going on in the world and I was being strangled by a three-inch flap of bed sheet. I could feel the back of my throat arching to gag. That was really all I needed. Calm down there, fellow, I told my throat. There was just one thing to do but it was entirely counterintuitive, like hitting serves with a backhand grip. I had to push out the little air that was left in my lungs and hope it dislodged the cloth. Otherwise anybody who had uses in mind for me was going to be disappointed.

I pushed.

The cloth gave way. The gagging was replaced

by a feathery tickle, which was probably not more than the seventh most unpleasant thing I had ever felt in my life.

Ever so carefully I pulled in air through my nose. It was good air. I mean, it smelled like oil and rubber and mildew, which made it a kind of enriched air. I liked it. I thought what a bizarre piece of machinery the body was, constantly sucking in air, taking a dab of oxygen out of it, then pushing it out again, most of the time without your even having to think about it. I just hoped I didn't have to cough.

I was beginning to feel a little irritation with the men in the car. If only they knew how well I could behave with only a sack over my head.

What I did then was to send a little imaginary Inspector General out to inspect every area of my body. He decided that I would survive the rap on the head. He shook his head sadly about the gag, but decided I would probably make it if we weren't going too far. He found by careful experimentation that my left foot could move almost six inches and my right hand could pronate and supernate up to 90 percent of its normal range. There were several hundred miles between my right knee and my forehead, but he crossed them like Lawrence crossing Aqaba to make his report.

I tried to tell myself that it was just a modification of the normal human condition. Normally human beings cannot fly or leave the surface of the planet, and they are restricted to living in areas with moderate temperature. So much of what is really out there they have to pick up indirectly. I realized that a sudden jab in my back was slowing down. Pressure on my kidneys was speeding up. Turns were experienced as pressure on the side of the neck.

I heard a truck horn and something that sounded like a whistle. There was a series of rapid turns, and then, an instant before I did, the car stopped. Doors opened and slammed, first nearby and then farther away. I heard the hiss of hydraulic brakes. Time passed. I was really starting to get mad. It was one thing to zonk me on the head and stuff me in a car trunk, but stopping for coffee and a sandwich was something else. My head was really starting to hurt, too.

They started out again, and every little turn did something new to my head and bladder. The bladder was really starting to worry me. I had invented a new type of gyroscope. My body was acutely attuned to changes in momentum. My bladder was also a kind of clock. I pictured it as a sort of hourglass that was getting fuller and fuller. They turned off on what must have been a bumpy country road, and that did it. The hourglass was ready to flip. About forty-five seconds later they stopped. Isn't that always the way?

The mouth of the whale opened, and Jonah was dragged forth. It was Crewcut who rolled me out onto the ground and gave me the kick in the kidneys. "You bastard, you peed in my car trunk!"

There is no pleasing some people. I was resigned to it.

"Not yet," another voice said.

Too late. There was another dull thud somewhere in the area of my head. Left ear this time.

When I came around I was in a small square room with a single light bulb. The only furniture was one of the tables they use for fall registration and a couple of straight-back kitchen chairs of the kind that young married couples buy at Sears. Crewcut and Princeton seemed to know their business, all right. This was what it was supposed to look like. They didn't get high marks for originality, though.

Princeton was busy doing something. Crewcut was leaning on his elbows watching me. I tried a smile to establish contact. I turned my head as far as it would go from left to right. I was tied to the chair in such a way that a full turn was painful. I thought I had indicated interest in the room.

"Cliché," I said.

Crewcut got up very slowly with no display of emotion.

"Want to try me with what this is all about?" It was getting hard to maintain eye contact. Eye contact, I knew, is a vital part of human interaction.

Crewcut was walking deliberately to a bag of some sort, which was just at the edge of my view.

"How was the snack at the truck stop?" I tried again. By now he was somewhere behind me, entirely out of my view. "I'm partial to the club sandwiches," I said. "I've found that truck stops do very well with club sandwiches."

The blow fell on my left bicep. It hardly made any sound at all. Whatever material the weapon was made out of had low vibration and/or great acoustical absorbency. The same was apparently true of my arm. I wondered if the element of surprise was what had made it hurt so much.

"Sorry," I said. "No hostile levity intended." At least I started to say that. I don't think I got to "levity" before the blow fell on my right deltoid. It's probably just as well; there are people who take offense at Latinate words.

I tried about an eight count of saying nothing at all. No dice. The blow caught my right shoulder blade. There was definitely something to the unexpectedness, but the pure pain was nothing to sneeze at either.

He was nothing if not systematic. He was in no hurry at all. He also had a good feel for randomness. His interval ranged from about a five count to one instance where I got to seventeen. Then again, I may have rushed the count.

What do you think of while you are being systematically beaten up? I thought about Dai Uy Han whacking away on his suspected VC. That was probably where Crewcut had gotten his training. I also thought of Karna and his people, who by comparison were really gents. Then I had a very bad thought. Crewcut and Princeton didn't seem to much mind if I saw their faces. By conventional wisdom, this is a bad sign. I mean, I was perfectly willing to quit at any point and no hard feelings, but how could I convince them I felt that way?

"Ready?" I heard the voice behind me. I wasn't, but I looked up and Princeton was standing in the door and nodding.

"One more for pissing in my car," the voice said.

There was another interval and then a shock wave ran up my right arm. It took me a minute to figure out that something had hit the point of my elbow. Princeton was holding up his hand like Michael Ansara in *Broken Arrow*.

I thought better of greeting him with "How!"

"You want something," I said.

Princeton gave me a hard look, then looked over to where Crewcut must be. "Do we *want* something?" he asked.

"Do we *want* something?"

Crewcut had wandered back into my field of vision, and he had the truncheon already raised when Princeton's wagging finger said to wait. Princeton had moved to the edge of my vision, and now he was fumbling around with something in the black bag. I started a guessing game about what it might be. Cattle prods were high on the list. I had seen one of those in use at Dai Uy Han's. Also bamboo slivers. Or a hand-carved board for beating the soles of the feet.

"Do we *want* something," Princeton muttered.

In that split second I made my decision. Whatever it was, I wasn't going to give it to them. You could either cooperate or not. It was a simple choice. In either case, they were going to torture me and kill me. I was going to become one with the bones of Jimmy Hoffa.

But they weren't going to get whatever they wanted. I think it was a combination of leaving me in the trunk at the truck stop and never bothering to ask first nicely. They would have done it the same way if they had *known* I was claustrophobic. They weren't nice. They lacked empathy.

"Well, you aren't getting anything from me," I said.

Princeton was unperturbed. He had emerged from the black bag and was approaching me with a long, slender implement in his hand. It was a hypodermic needle.

25.
A Trip with Emily

Luckily I don't much mind needles. In fact, I used to take a certain pride in watching the football behemoths fall out from army inoculations.

"Ready?" Princeton said.

"At your pleasure," I answered.

But nobody talked to me anymore. He was talking to Crewcut, who moved around to grab me by the arms.

I took a deep breath. I had never seen the application of drugs. Dai Uy Han's methods had been more elemental. I wondered if they had been used in North Vietnam. I remembered reading that the Americans who had resisted torture had been men of strong convictions, usually religious, combined with strong constitutions. I had some doubts about my own convictions.

"You're gonna like it at first," Crewcut said. "Then you're gonna hate it."

Princeton got the needle into the vein like a pro, credit him with that. I was grasping at any evidence of professionalism. I had to hope that he knew the proper dosage.

For a minute there was nothing at all. Or maybe just a little tingling in the hands and feet, which could have been nothing but nerves.

Then it hit me with a rush.

Except for the little warm spot in my chest, I felt good. I felt incredibly good. I was hungry as a spring bear and ready to have sex with a hole in the wall. I felt super incredibly good.

Suddenly I felt *too* good.

My body was burning away out of control and my mind couldn't seem to stop it. My heart was racing like the kettledrum solo in *Also Sprach Zarathustra*.

"What?" I asked. "What did you give me?"

It came out in a low shaky voice that sounded like whayogimme?

The kettledrum had slowed down now, but it was playing in some sort of echo chamber. BOOM! BOOM! BOOM!

"You've had a little combo of sensory enhancers," Princeton said. "Things you like the feel of will feel really good. Things you don't like, you will really hate."

I decided I didn't like the way my heart was pounding. I was also feeling very warm, especially in my chest.

"Now let's have a little talk about Frank Cole," Princeton said. He was floating on the edge of the table across about forty kilometers of ocean floor. He must have been at least the size of Godzilla.

"Don' know any Coles," I said. "No kohlrabis, either." For some reason I struck myself as terrifically funny. I mean, my tickle box turned over. I laughed until my heart rate jumped another twenty beats.

Crewcut was not amused. I saw the punch approaching the side of my head like a docking spaceship. It made contact with a loud clang. All I felt was pain.

My heart joined in the celebration. BOOOM! BOOOM! BOOOM!

There was a low sound, like a fluorescent light or a radio between channels. Or a fly, a ragged, late-summer fly. I heard a fly buzz when I died. Now where was that from?

"You are being difficult, Mr. McCallum. We know that you have been making inquiries into the affairs of Frank Cole. We also know that you are in possession of a document which concerns Mr. Cole. Now if you will just tell us the whereabouts of this document, we can be done with this inconvenience."

It came to me like a released prisoner.

"Emily Dickinson," I blurted.

"Yes, go on, Mr. McCallum."

"The fly," I said. "The buzz."

"Did you give him too much?" Crewcut said.

"Nah, he's still playing games," Princeton said. A low-flying 727 came by with that peculiar aluminum-plastic engine sound and the whoosh of displaced air. Its landing gear caught the crown of my head.

"I felt a funeral in my brain," I said woozily.

There was a new thing I didn't care much for. I shivered. I was starting to feel cold. I was feeling really cold. I didn't like the heartbeat interval either. There were about fifteen or twenty seconds between BOOMS.

"Why don't you tell us the location of the document?" Princeton started in again. It had been a long time now between BOOMS. I thought that was a bad sign. Also, my teeth were chattering. They chattered so hard it made my head hurt. I waited, and finally there was a faint boom.

"Because I could not stop for death," I said.

The 727 was coasting into the terminal where I waited. It crashed right through the glass, and the left wing caught me in the mouth. I tasted rich, salty, beefy blood. I was also doing a backward half gainer.

It was not death, for I stood up. Threw up, too. Puko, ergo sum. That seemed to steady my heart rate a bit. Don't hope, I told myself. The thing with feathers that perches in the soul.

Crewcut was laying me across the table like a cadaver. Princeton was holding another hypodermic. I didn't remember his refilling it. There was a certain slant of light: about 300 watts.

"You'll talk," Princeton said. "In the end we'll get everything we want."

"Success is counted sweetest," I said, "by those who ne'er succeed."

* * *

While I was fearing it, it came. This time there
was a surge of nausea, followed by a rapid shrinking
of the room. As far as I could tell, I wasn't even tied
down, but my hands wouldn't move. The room was
getting so small it was starting to feel like the car
trunk. The walls were moving in really fast.

"Whooaa!" I said.

The wall wasn't listening, so what I finally did
was picture myself nailing up beams to keep the
room from shrinking. I managed to hold it at about
4 by 4 by 4.

Sometimes Princeton did the questioning while
Crewcut did the beating, and then after a while they
would switch over. I think deep down Princeton was
the hypodermic and questioning specialist and
Crewcut was the hitting specialist, but even Crewcut
occasionally got tired. I had heard that Green Berets
were cross-trained in several specialties. My life closed
twice before its close. About five months passed.

After a while Princeton held up a paper he had
taken from my wallet. "Who is this Laura Westin?"

I laughed a crumbling laugh.

"You may as well tell us," he said. "I expect we'll
get the whole story from this Laura person anyway."

That was when I almost told them. It seemed
somehow wrong, though, after getting this far. Crewcut summoned the strength to hit me a few more
times, and then he was no longer in the room. But
then neither was I. I don't know where I was.

26.
Dinner with Pedro

When I got back to the surface, I could hear Princeton talking in the next room. There were silences, so he had to be on the telephone. That meant Crewcut was still out trying to get satisfaction out of Laura Westin, and good luck to them both. She would have to take care of herself for the moment, and so would he. The light was still pelting down into my dilated pupils, and there was no being sure whether it was night or day or how many hours they had held me there. I was feeling a little punk in general, to say nothing of places on my head and arms where I had been hit, but several body parts seemed capable of moving. It gradually came to me that they had not even bothered to tie me down.

Now that really grated. I may have been a university professor, but I prided myself in the idea that I was not a total and unmitigated wimp. What it did, really, was to give me lots and lots of motivation. I levered my upper body to a sitting position. It was sort of like raising the wall of a barn with levers and pulleys, but once I got there I didn't feel all that much worse. Princeton was still chatting away on the telephone. When talking to a friend, he didn't really sound like that bad a guy. Leaving me untied was probably just carelessness. He didn't seem like an insult adder. He had been careless about the hypodermic needle too.

It was sitting on top of his little kit about eight nautical miles away. The room had gotten big again. Leaving it untended that way was the kind of thing people did whom life had taught to be overconfident. I let myself down from the table slowly and crawled toward it on hands and knees. I wasn't quite ready for takeoff to full standing position.

It was one hell of a needle. I think it must have been the kind they use to inoculate cows and horses. His bag was full of little jars of liquid, some labeled and some not. It mattered scant as I didn't understand the labels anyway. I just took a bit of this and a bit of that. I was sorry, but when you drop in unexpectedly you take potluck. I filled it to the brim.

All I really had to do now was get up enough rev to come to my feet and make a lunge. I had energy for about one, so there was no rehearsal. Mentally, I went over what the sergeants at basic had said about bayonet thrust and parry. I also pictured those Japanese assassins leaping up on stages to hit some industrialist in the chest. Also a fencer I knew in college. Épée, I think. So many things in life are merely variations on a theme. I stood flat in the corner, using the side wall for leverage. About fifteen seconds after the telephone receiver was replaced, Princeton stepped through the door and my lunge caught him between the fourth and fifth ribs. I pushed the plunger in to the hilt. It went in so far the hypodermic broke off in the struggle.

He had a terrifically surprised look on his face, but he was still strong enough to push me on my back with one arm. I think it was his other arm that broke off the needle. He held it up in his hand as if seeing it truly for the first time, then he looked over to where I was sitting on the floor and said, "You little booger." He was in the process of sliding down the wall himself, which turned him into my exact mirror image.

"You little booger," he said again.

"Eat shit," I said.

It struck him as funny. I decided it was pretty comical too.

"Hey, you think that was funny, get this one. This cowboy walks into a bar, see, and they ask him if he has ever met Pedro Gonzales. Have I ever met Pedro Gonzales? he says. Have I ever met Pedro Gonzales?"

Princeton was just continuing to laugh in a low whuffing sound that was sort of like a cough. I decided that he really wasn't a bad fellow at all.

"So the cowboy tells the story of how Pedro jumped out from behind a rock and held him up. Drop your guns, Pedro says, and he drops his guns. Then Pedro says get off your horse, so he gets off his horse. Then Pedro says take down your pants, so he takes down his pants. 'Then Pedro says sheet, and I sheet. Then Pedro says eat it, so I ate it.' "

Now I don't mind people anticipating my punch lines, but Princeton was just going wild. He was laughing like a sick hyena, hugging his chest all the time with his free hand while the broken needle dangled in his other.

"You think that's funny," I said. He was really a boon companion, a Prince. "The cowboy goes on with his story. 'So Pedro laughs so hard he drops his gun, and I pick it up and point it at him and say now you get down from the horse, and he gets down. Then I say drop your gunbelt, and he drops it. Then I say take down your pants, and he takes them down. Then I say sheet, and he sheets. Then I say eat it, and he eats it.' "

Princeton was whuffing so hard by now that it was like a series of small convulsions, but I didn't much like the gray that was creeping into his face.

"Wait for the punch line," I say. "So the cowboy turns to his friend at the bar and says, Hell, you ask me if I know Pedro Gonzales? Hell, I had dinner with him."

Princeton was still whuffing, but the sense of mirth had somehow gone out of it. He gave me a look that told me we maybe weren't going to be the buddies I thought. "Eat shit and die, then," I said.

A kind of slow smile spread over his face and his eyes settled into a stare. I crawled over and checked his pulse. He had achieved nirvana. I wasn't feeling much pain myself. Something about active living had given the drugs another pump through my system.

I got the feeling you get when you laugh too hard too late in the party. A kind of gray veil came down and my cheek was against the floor, which was varnished wood with a pretty good buildup of dust and varnish in the cracks.

When I came around again, strange things were going on around me. I was hearing odd things. People were talking in a foreign language that sounded a lot like Russian. One of them was saying a lot of things like foolski, and idiotski, and stupid son of a bitchski. The other one was the one who took my pulse.

"Is he dead?" his friend asked.

"Nyet."

"Will he die?"

"Nyet."

Was I relieved? *Da.* But I noticed that the one who spoke pidgin Russian also spoke English. The one who spoke good Russian probably spoke pidgin English. That's why he answered in Russian. It was very interesting. I stole one quick glance, then shut my eyes. They were scrambling around making a good bit of racket, but I had made up my mind that nothing repeat nothing was going to get me to wake up.

They were also conducting a conversation in that funny kind of pidgin English/pidgin Russian of two people who are not entirely comfortable in each other's languages. Now my Russian isn't that good, either, but I could tell that the main point of contention was something black. *Chyornee,* that is. *Korobka,* I thought maybe.

You have to watch Russian idioms. When American astronomers first discovered the things they called "black holes," there had been a small scientific scandal. Whoever translated the journals into Russian did it literally. In Russian, the expression "black hole," is not used in polite company until after three or four vodkas. So what on earth was a *chyornee korobka,* a black box?

· When I woke up finally, with a dry swollen tongue, headache, receding nausea, and the hangover feeling of being a strange interloper on the planet, the room was deserted. No Princeton, no needles. No ropes, no little black bags, no evidence of illness or death. If they were trying to persuade me I had just been on a bender, they had missed a couple of points, though.

Two of my front teeth were loose. I was going to have bruises over much of my body, and on parts invisible to the naked eye. I was getting cold again, too, but this was because somebody had remembered to turn down the heat. I was wearing all my clothes except my overcoat, although they had gotten my underwear on backward. My wallet was on the registration table. I checked the contents. They hadn't been after money or credit cards, as Marlowe would have observed. The sheet with Laura Westin's address was still missing.

After great pain, a formal feeling comes. It carried me back to certain epic student hangovers. I had a sense of painful rebirth. The rediscovery of self and the world, a certain Renaissance scholar had called it.

The ceiling had receded to eight feet or so, which seemed just about right, but I checked it on a minute-to-minute basis. I could pretty much hold it there with nothing but strong conviction and a cheerful attitude. My nerve endings had enjoyed better moments, my head hurt bad, my arms and legs were shaking, and I couldn't shake the afteraura. I was also worried about Laura Westin.

I managed to stagger outside and tasted a liquor never brewed. If they could only find a way to bill you for clean country air. It was an old farmhouse, not more than a half mile off Highway 20 fifteen miles south of Freeport, and as good a location for a KGB safe house as you would ever find. Close enough to the consulate, but well out of earshot of any neighbors. It didn't take longer than three hours to get an old farmer in a pickup to stop for me. By then I was shaking a little less, but I was careful not to let him have a look at my face until the open door had established an implicit contract. He was wise in the ways of the world.

"One too many?"

I nodded soberly. I had learned my lesson good.

He let me off at the bus station in Freeport, and I was pleased that the woman in pale green would serve me a cup of coffee. I took it in careful little sips while stealing a glance at her *Sun-Times*. When she left to tend to another customer, I'm afraid I was rude enough to turn it around.

The woman who shot the burglar was being released on her own recognizance. The only thing that bothered the state's attorney had to do with the origin of the pistol. Her victim had turned out to be an ex-Green Beret and three-tour Vietnam vet named Joe Hennessey. He had been decorated for valor and was assumed to be suffering from that posttraumatic syndrome that led so many Viet vets to tragically antisocial behavior. It was a sad thing all around.

Public response had been generally sympathetic to the woman and it was the fear that she might become some kind of public hero that was leading the state's attorney to proceed so carefully. She had been sitting up reading when she heard the prowler. She went for the .38, which had been a bequest from her woodpecker-shooting grandfather. (How was she supposed to keep up with registration laws, and how could they expect her elderly grandmother to have registered it either?) She had just waited calmly on the sofa with the gun beneath a cushion. You heard so many horror stories about rape these days, and they didn't even seem to care about age. There was a fresh picture of Laura Westin leaving court, looking plucky and indomitable and about seventy. I could imagine how much it annoyed her to dowdify herself that way, even to such a good purpose. There was an old picture of Crewcut in his green beanie. The only thing that had tempered the sympathy a bit was the fact that she had kept firing. Six shots might strike some milk-and-water types as excessive force. It had been duly noted that not one of them had missed.

27.
Note from
the Dead

Maybe I could have quit right there and cashed in my chips. Then again maybe I couldn't. I had killed one man, whom somebody cared about if only his mother, and I felt responsible for the deaths of three others. Two of them were my friends, and the third had my fingerprints on his mailbox and screen door. Besides, Sorel says the greatest mistake the amateur makes is to sell just as the market is finally beginning to turn up.

I spent the night in a flophouse off Maxwell Street and resisted the temptation to call Laura Westin. By now she had either written me off as unchivalrous, or she was already saying rosaries or whatever she said. The person I thought it just might be safe to call was Sorel. He was in his office bright and early, waiting to give the clerks and flunkies the look that said that was why he was where he was and they were where they were. He had missed me yesterday at racquetball—I mean when you get up at six getting stood up is no small thing—but he had understood when he saw the morning paper. He said we could meet around ten at the entrance to the trading floor. By then the markets would have reacted to overnight trading in Europe.

The boy who checked my pass didn't say a word. You would have thought people came in with black eyes and multiple contusions every day. They probably did.

"Hey, that's a hell of a shiner," Sorel said. He seemed to think it was some sort of an achievement to get your head busted.

"You should see the other guy," I said. Sorel was handing me a pass.

"Come watch the bonds run," he said. "Oil futures are about to crack."

We sauntered by a couple of stations. Traders stopped to nod at Sorel. He gave some of them a pat on the back and others a poke in the chest. Nobody noticed the shiner.

"How's Laura?" I asked.

"As good as can be expected," he said. "To tell the truth, she wouldn't have missed it. She takes the popular view of burglars. Shoot first, six or eight times."

"What about the state's attorney?"

"No sweat. You don't get reelected in Cook County by prosecuting helpless little old ladies. The ones who are being a little hard-core about it are ATF."

"ATF?"

"Alcohol, Tobacco, and Firearms. Department of the Treasury. They're the people who guarantee the soundness of your money and make sure the Mafia is no better armed than platoons of heavy infantry."

"I would have thought they would be frying larger fish than unregistered Smith and Wesson thirty-eights," I said.

"Laura was sort of thinking the same way," Sorel said.

I gave Sorel the postcard version of what had happened to me. He was giving orders, mainly to buy bond futures, between nods, but when I was done he gave the shiner a second look. When I told him what I needed, he gave me the key to his apartment and told me where to put it when I was done. Then he reached for his wallet and peeled off five crisp hundred-dollar bills. It was nice to know I had a friend with five C-notes of lending money on his person at a given time. It was even nicer to know that there was somebody left in the world who placed my total value at as much as five hundred dollars that he would probably never see again.

What I did first with the five hundred dollars was go to Saks and buy a couple of suits and some dark glasses. Also a dark warmup suit. That is, I didn't pay with the C-notes. What I did was use them as a prop so the clerk wouldn't mind taking my credit card. He didn't notice my shiner either, not even while I was picking out the dark glasses. He sold them to me as if I were about to go for a vacation to the islands. It was part of my continuing education in the fact that people with money to spend have no physical defects.

I used Sorel's apartment to change and get cleaned up. I borrowed one of his more modest endangered-animal valises and a rare-species belt. As far as Sorel was concerned, the Department of the Interior kept these lists purely as a courtesy to the European designers. I was sorry that we didn't wear the same shoe size. I copped his number three or four backup cologne and shaving accessories, too.

The five C-notes were really for taxis and the use of pay toilets as necessary. I took one to the library, yes, the library, please don't talk, I practice meditation, and had him wait. He did it for only a five-dollar deposit, which goes to show that even behind shades and swollen cheekbones I have a face that a common man can recognize as honest.

I didn't even have to bother with the card catalog. A library is one of those rare oases in life that remain in perfect rational order; when the terrorists begin sneaking into libraries and reshelving books out of sequence, it will truly be the end of a civilizing process that began with Aristotle. My only fear was that someone might have checked out the book, but with the sloth of the present generation of undergraduates I needed have no fear.

The World of Humanism begins with the assertion of Aeneas Silvius Piccolomini (Pope Pius II, according to Gilmore, and who can doubt him?, one of the best informed men in Europe) that in the year 1453 all of the West was on the brink of falling apart. That it did not, Gilmore attributes to the energy of European pluralism and the vitality imparted by the rediscovery of humanistic learning. In this latter half of the twentieth century, one sought comfort where he could find it. The note from Max was placed carefully between pages 218 and 219, a fact that had no significance beyond the obvious, that this location provided the maximum adhesion in case the book was moved and seemed the most impervious to casual student perusal. The note said more or less exactly what I knew it must.

28.
Cross-References

My friend,

You have provided me with a consummate challenge—a challenge which, within the constraints of the time and resources allotted, has allowed me to use my modest talent to the utmost. For this I thank you. I look forward to explaining in full the reasoning and procedures employed. This morning, however, Miss Peabody reported strange visitors and I thought it prudent to invoke the backup procedure upon which we agreed. There are no records of my search, either on paper or in computer storage. The details reside only in that organic database that is so difficult for rival researchers to access, although I do not doubt that my process can be replicated by a skilled researcher of kindred mind.

Should the occasion arise, you should know something of my sources. My point of departure was the General Accounting Office Annual Audit for the years 1946 to the present, with special attention to the changes in reporting format introduced in 1975. You may recall that the deliberations of the Church Committee took place around that time.

The *Congressional Record*, 1946–1974, was of passing utility, and the microfilm files of *The New York Times*, with their careful index, were indispensable. You might have a look at the tabular data appended in Swain and Andrews, *Management and Organization of Federal Agencies.* SEC filings between 1970 and 1981 were an early and necessary source. They will lead naturally and inevitably to certain readily available corporate annual reports.

If I were to publish my results (a regrettable impossibility, I realize) I would be compelled to cite K. A. McCallum's "The Use of Foreign Service Rosters in the Determination of Informal Job Function" (alas, also unpublished), a seminal work that displays both originality and sagacity in its grasp of the cross-referencing technique. McCallum's work provided a key in closing several gaps in the material.

A regression analysis of statistical divergence in foreign-service career patterns just prior to retirement will provide a startling insight. (Ref: *Who's Who, Who Was Who,* McKeon's *State Department Biographies,* and Martin and Ashare's *Analysis of Career Pattern in Foreign Service Functional Cones.*) A study of career military officers taking early retirement without passover produces a strikingly similar result.

But so much for technique. The results are quite enlightening.

The supervision of proprietaries and purveyors must be performed operationally under a special logistical section laterally related to (and funded under) the Director of Internal Review. The Inspector General has oversight responsibility. The regional and line sections are involved on an ad hoc basis, and special departments must apply for liaison as special requirements arise. This compartmentalization of cover entities holds true except when usage is so widespread as to make it infeasible.

Foundations and corporations are treated in similar fashion. The standing procedure must specify the control of proprietaries through the use of former case officers and "contract" employees—"family," I believe, being the colloquialism. There is a preference for the combined use of one insider and one outsider. The identity of the outside controller is in theory not known to the host organization, although in many cases it must be evident. The insider has line responsibility.

The virtue of this procedure is to construct a system of check and countercheck, in which either of the two men is in position to report malfeasance on the part of the other. It is a bit like killing the killers of the gravediggers who bury the Pharaoh, is it not?

You see, the outside source may be privy to information the company wishes to conceal from the Agency. In actuality, all major purveyors and proprietaries must be well aware of the system, although that in itself is a safeguard of sorts. But what if the two controlling agents were to be in cahoots? Oh, well.

It is gratifying, if somewhat alarming, to realize

that all of the above information was derived in a few days of work from the resources of a single university library. Are we quite safe in this country? Let us hope, at least, that our enemies, whoever they may be, are not in good supply of skilled bibliophiles. Of course there is no ironclad means of corroborating the above suppositions, but one's best corroboration is often intuition, is it not? And I can say this much: If I were instituting a system of logistical and cover organizations for an intelligence organization, this is how I would go about it.

But what are you up to, old friend? Miss Peabody was distinctly unnerved by her visitors, and old Thistlethwaite said there was something in their manner that prompted him to lock up the manuscript room. What have we uncovered? No doubt we shall share a laugh about this over tea at the Nonesuch, but I am sufficiently impressed with the company you have attracted to put this rather preposterous system of communication into effect. As always, you have provided my drab life with its small quantum of spice. •

Max

Of course it could not have been otherwise. What I had really come to hear was Max's voice, refusing all contractions and putting every colloquialism into invisible italics. It was the little push I needed to see things through. The cabby dropped me off at the United terminal and spake never a word about my shiner. Neither did the ticket agent, who turned out to be perfectly willing to provide a trip to San Francisco in return for an impression made by a little plastic card.

29.
Burglar

Marlowe would just have jumped into a car and taken a quick drive over to the address on a slip of paper, or at the very worst grabbed a boat, which goes to show how times change. I took a taxi from San Francisco International. I didn't bother stopping at Pacair this time. What I needed would be at Allbright's house if it existed at all.

The cabby crept around to the side street where they hide the on ramp to the Golden Gate Bridge. I wanted to pay it close attention this time. It's one of those wonders of the world that when you are actually there, you can't quite believe this is it. By the time you accept that it is, you are seeing the signs for San Rafael and it is over. It's much more convincing from an airplane.

He dropped me off two houses down from Allbright's. I don't know quite how I expected to handle it. A simple burglary, I suppose. No tools, no expertise, no experience, but that's how it is with intellectual dilettantes. It was the way things were headed in my life. First you kill a man, then you commit burglaries. Before you know it, you get tempted to pad expenses on your income tax.

It wasn't going to be that easy a house to burgle, but I was in luck because a second-story bathroom window was open a crack and the access was hidden by a hedge of spruce trees from all but those with binoculars on Alcatraz. I could probably have made it without the skills acquired the summer I went climbing in the Rockies.

The bathroom had lots of female toiletries of the expensive kind that single women acquire when they are very concerned about the first impression they are going to make on men. On the other hand, they were mixed up with Allbright's soap and razors thoroughly enough that she was probably planning on an extended stay.

She had a room of her own with three summer stewardess uniforms and eight summer dresses hanging in the closet, along with nineteen belts and twenty-two pairs of shoes. Allbright's bedroom had the double bed. He was a man after my own heart. There were four winter and three summer suits, and two of the winter suits appeared to be identical. He owned skis, mountain-climbing equipment, and three medium-priced mid-size graphite tennis rackets. There was an old M-2 carbine in the closet and a shotgun under the right-hand side of the bed, which was also the side with the reading lamp. Both barrels were loaded.

The bottom drawer of his work desk contained pictures of three wives with three sets of children, taken in lots of the same places as Leitsey's had been, but without the camels and elephants. There was also a picture of the Three Musketeers, Allbright, Princeton, Crewcut, and a tall but rather owlish man, all dressed in khakis. The furniture was made out of impermeable, undentable twentieth-century stuff. It was like a space lab, more or less, and Allbright had brought along about what an astronaut is allowed. His theory seemed to be that what you could really own in life was everything you were able to remember, plus a nice view.

I made my way downstairs carefully, although Allbright didn't seem the kind of man to own unsuspected pets. There were none. The living room contained more impermeable stuff, a TV set built into the wall, and the kind of artwork that interior decorators who are not complete flamers like to put on the walls of high-class motel chains. I paused to glance at the computer console in his den, but I was beginning to have bad presentiments.

I moved inexorably toward the kitchen where I hoped to find only soup cubes and jars of Tang, but where of course Allbright himself was, and may all the king's enemies ride as that young man rode. From the look of it, whoever shot him had been someone he knew well, or at least someone for whom he was willing to mix a couple of Allbright Slings. His head was lying in a sticky residue of blood and gin, and the entry wound in the back seemed the kind that might have been made by a small-bore pistol. I'm no Marlowe, but I guessed a .22.

Whoever did it had had complete confidence in his first shot, which from the exit wound must have been at point-blank range. My acquaintance with Allbright had been brief, far briefer than with Gus Friedler, but I couldn't help thinking of all the places he was going to be missed. What triggered the wave of nausea, though, was that evaporating film of gin.

I got to the front door, which was open, wouldn't you know, hesitated long enough to leave a set of smudged prints for the SFPD, and then remembered that I had a job to do. I had been pretty sure that there would be no papers, but the computer clinched it. It was a really nice Digital, the kind a person buys who really needs one and knows what he needs it *for*. I didn't know diddly about operating it, the one we have in the department is an IBM PC, but it was what they call in the trade user-friendly. I tried to smile as I hit the ON button.

I didn't know quite what I was looking for, but there are three or four basic commands and it didn't take me long to get the sort of data that I thought I wanted. Once I got it, I didn't know quite how to work with it, short a printer, but I called the people at DEC with a theoretical question and got a sales engineer who came up with a clever SEARCH program right off the top. You have to give those people credit. IBM had better be right on its toes.

What my SEARCH turned up was the short list of addresses in Allbright's personal duplicate list of shippings and billings that had suddenly stopped being billed and shipped to in the past three months. There were three leading contenders, one each in Jakarta, Manila, and Singapore. I had sort of lost conviction about the value of my Indonesia visa, and Manila could be a rough town too. Singapore was a nice orderly kind of place, and didn't require a visa of Americans in good standing with their own State Department (which I assumed I would still be pending the processing of a fair country stack of paperwork). Anyway, I just wanted to see Singapore. And with the help of the SEAAAC foundation, you can see the parts of the world you want to see.

I guess there was something telepathic about this last thought, for just at that moment the telephone rang. I picked it up, did my best to summon up a lusty hullo, and waited. After about ten seconds, a voice came on as clear as Oakland, without even a hint of an echo. "Bill, is that you? I've been frantic."

There was another ten-second delay, and the voice said, "Bill? That's not you, is it?"

"No," I said. "It's not Bill."

I didn't know what else to say.

30.
Utopia

Pacific Orient joined the group that didn't care how I looked, and so did Singapore customs and immigration. The busted-up look was in. Oh, I got a second glance in Singapore. Papa Lee is hard-core about one's personal appearance, and in the hippie era I had heard of kids getting sent for haircuts before they got their papers stamped. I guess I still looked like a guy who could pay his hotel bill.

Singapore is probably what the world is coming to best case, and you can make of it what you will. You can drink the water in Singapore, and you can also use it as a metaphor. They don't have any of it salt-free, so they import it from upcountry Malaysia, purify it, take what they need, and sell the rest back to the Malays at a small net profit. You can also drink the water in Malaysia.

Lee Kuan Yew was a man with a single idea,

and it is best translated as "You Occidentals ain't seen nothing yet." There is no poverty in Singapore except for that handful determined to remain picturesque. It is the Mercedes and Bentley capital of the world, bar not West Palm. But when you drive one into the center of town, you have got to have at least five people in it or pay a fine. It's like flying Lufthansa; everything is absolutely under control and every need will be tended to as long as you follow orders.

Now normally a visitor heads straight to Raffles, where he can mosey down at his leisure to have a sloe gin sling and conjure the ghost of Somerset Maugham. Personally, Raffles makes me feel like I am sleeping and drinking in a museum, or at the very least one of those houses protected by some little-old-lady society that won't let you move the furniture. I could also feel the hot breath of irritated real-estate developers through the cracks around the air conditioning. I mean, there's just so much wasted space up there in the air.

I checked into the Mandarin. It is a space capsule humanized by artificial bamboo, the air conditioning works perfectly, there are mirrors all around the lobby and restaurants, and the bar will serve you the same Singapore sling, or a Laphroaig, if you know how to say it. It also has one of those peculiar sundial pools you find halfway up a high-rise, with the sun slanting in to make interesting astronomical predictions around several severe Easter Island slabs of building.

I settled down with my Laphroaig of course no ice between a group of hairy Australians and a group of hairy Germans. The Germans seemed to be buyers and the Aussies sellers. A couple of families of Japanese arrived, businessmen with wives and children, and I watched them carefully select a location. The two men stood together and pointed at the various rocks of Stonehenge, and they seemed to have about worked out the time and place of the winter solstice when one of them turned and told the women where to place the mats. They weren't going to be cheated, these Japanese; they were going to collect their legal entitlement of sun.

When the lounge chairs were lined up in properly methodical fashion, they began the elaborate and rather awkward ritual of stripping off their robes. You could tell they didn't like this much from the way they held in their arms and elbows. The women were wearing bikinis, not skimpy bikinis but, well, bikinis, and they didn't look more than two thirds as silly as the dean's wife giving dinner parties in a kimono. They didn't like this sort of stuff, but it came with the computers and transistors and they were by God going to do it. The men had gone ahead to test the water, which I already knew was of a oneness with Baffin Bay, but I didn't want to discourage them. The eldest male tried it first with his toe, and was followed by each of the others in order to the youngest female. There was more discussion, some more pointing at buildings and sun, and then the eldest male walked to the end of the diving board and executed a technically flawless and entirely graceless dive. The others followed by rank. Kamikazes. As they stepped out of the pool, their leader stole a glance at the Aussie salesmen. They had made those dives for Japan.

I was beginning to be pleasantly drowsy, so I downed the warm Laphroaig and allowed myself to doze off. I hardly noticed the middle-aged American who had made them open the poolside bar. When I woke up the pool area was in full shadow and I had goose bumps. It was all deserted but for the gin-drinking American and myself, and the waiters were giving him dirty looks. I told myself it couldn't possibly be the same gin and tonic. As I walked to the elevators, he gave me a slight nod, but didn't get up. I gave him a nod back. Now you tell me how it is you can always identify a fellow Yank?

Straits Technology was located in one of the newer *ang mos,* built over the demolition of a Malay *kampong* just behind the airport. I had put on my black warm-up suit but not gone so far as to shoe-black my face or tennis shoes. A person can carry professionalism too far. I had splurged on another Rent-A-Car, and that is how I made my first reconnaissance.

It was all part of a larger complex, and what I was hoping was that they had economized and decided to go together on a single security guard. The construction of the fence suggested it strongly, and anyway you can never prove the negative, as they say. The front and sides of the compound were well lighted, but the back was flush with the Johore Strait, and I suspected there might be useful irregularities of terrain, if only for illegal dumping of waste.

Recon by foot told me that I was right, and I was growing more and more confident about the security guard. After all, who would be stealing from them when it was they who were doing the stealing?

Just the same I was happy to find a dark place between lights where a bit of erosion let me go under rather than over the wire. I walked directly to the warehouse that had to be Straits Technology with not a sign of human security and stuck my head around to the front just to be sure it was clear and to read the sign on the door. I am sorry to say that what I did then was to vandalize a window, although it was the smallest and looked the easiest to repair of the windows on the side. To tell the truth, the building did not have an overabundance of windows, and absolutely none of them was prebroken.

I got over the side with only a slight tear in my warm-up from jagged glass and my flashlight began immediately to spy out a most wonderful concept of science fiction. There all around me were long tables of assembly lines, only in reverse. It was as if some mad genius were hard at work uninventing the world. He had started with computers and VCRs and the latest electronic gadgets and was probably working his way backward toward the radio and the telephone and finally the wheel. Anyway backward was the word for it.

Computers seemed to be what he was stuck on right now, although there were a number of other electronic gadgets that had no obvious function but a lot of very high-powered wiring. One of them reminded me a little bit of the inner workings of those big Pratt & Whitney jets. The favorite among computers seemed to be the Apple. There were six of them in various stages of disassembly. I also saw several Tandys stacked against a wall, as if the mad scientist weren't quite ready to uninvent them yet, and some IBMs that were only partially uncrated. There was even one of my very own little DEC, the one in which I had found the name and address of this company.

Nor had Gyro Gearloose neglected the small things. When I took the trouble to look more closely, I saw the tables with microscopes and microscopic implements and the little chips and miniature parts and instruments. I should have known. When you set out to uninvent the world, you have to organize and coordinate carefully. It wouldn't do to uninvent the computer and leave all those memory chips lying around without any use. The world of science doesn't work that way.

All kidding aside, what I was looking at had to be one of the largest reverse-engineering installations in all Southeast Asia. I knew all about reverse engineering because I read *The Wall Street Journal*. The general idea was to produce cheap knock-offs of pirated consumer products, but there was also a steady effort to steal genuine high technology. I was just beginning to consider what I was actually going to do with this new information when lights started switching on. They had probably been turned on by the darkish man in white tagalog shirt who was pointing an automatic pistol at my midsection.

He used the pistol to direct me into an office with S. RAMANUJAN engraved on the door. "Right here, sir, while I decide whether I will be more seriously inconvenienced by shooting you as you flee or allowing Mr. Lee to put you under the jail. Here in Singapore we take industrial espionage very seriously."

"I can see that," I said.

I admired his Oxonian English, you can really only find it these days in Bombay, but I noted that it turned the sir into a punctuation mark. "If you shoot me, you will never have the benefit of my knowledge," I said. I was measuring the distance between us very carefully and trying to remember what the sergeant in basic training had said about this kind of situation. It had always seemed to me that a properly executed kick ought to be faster than a trigger squeeze. Ought to be. Should be. But was that what they said in Hand-to-Hand, or was it an illusion of the kicker's point of view?

I was about to put it to the test when I heard the door open and a second figure appeared with pointed gun. He had a wallet open to some sort of shield in his other hand, and I could see the pith helmets of uniformed Singapore police bobbing over his shoulder.

"Gerald Pafko, ATF," he introduced himself.

"If that's the teacher union, I'm not interested," I said.

"Alcohol, Tobacco, and Firearms," he explained.

"Don't look at me," I said. "I don't believe I've ever run afoul of the tobacco laws."

"You may go ahead and arrest him," Pafko said to the leader of the pith helmets. I held my hands out for the handcuffs, but at the same time Ramanujan slowly lowered his pistol. The pith helmet walked straight across the room and put handcuffs on Ramanujan.

I was surprised how many common friends and interests Pafko and I turned out to have. He knew all about Hamer, and when I said I didn't do it, truly, he didn't doubt me for a minute. He had also received word about Allbright from the San Francisco office. He didn't think I needed be overly concerned about the fingerprints. It was his opinion that both Hamer and Allbright were likely to become additions to the list of unsolved crimes, of which there were no more than seven or eight hundred thousand in a single year. He had gotten a bang out of Laura Westin and very much regretted having had to be stern with her. He described a man very much like Princeton who was still among the missing and speculated that his body might well turn up in due time. I couldn't help him there. He didn't bat an eye at the mention of Frank Cole.

He assured me that I had never been in any real danger from Ramanujan, who was, after all, a Hindu as well as a a physicist.

I don't say that Pafko just opened up and started telling me things right away. In fact, for the first couple of hours at Police Headquarters he seemed wary and spoke of calling in the embassy people in the morning. He kept trying to call his office and not getting through. Then when he got through his attitude toward me seemed to change, not that I had suddenly become a better person but that I had suddenly become irrelevant. The reason was on the back page of that morning's *Straits Times*.

31.
Death of a Cold Warrior

ROME (AP)—A former American intelligence officer was shot dead this morning by an unknown assailant as he waited to change planes at Rome's Leonardo da Vinci airport. American officials on the scene identified the slain officer as Francis S. K. Cole, allegedly a former agent of the Central Intelligence Agency. Cole had been under investigation on suspicion of providing illegal arms and technology to Libya. At the time of the shooting Cole was apparently in transit from Tripoli. A spokesman for Italian authorities disclosed that Cole was in possession of two passports, one in his own name and one in the name of Scott Kirby. He also held an Aeroflot ticket to Moscow in the name of Kirby.

Cole was reported to have been a senior officer on the covert side of the CIA until his retirement several years ago. There was speculation that Cole's movement from Tripoli was part of an elaborate sting operation by American law enforcement agencies in cooperation with SID, frustrated in the event by an unknown third party.

George Jonas, a political officer at the U.S. Embassy, denied that Cole was an undercover intelligence operative, but confirmed that his activities in Libya had drawn the attention of American law enforcement groups. (See story page 3, Britain expels two Soviet cultural aides on charges of espionage.)

There was a head shot of Cole looking bald and old and harmless, the way obituary photographs often look. I noticed something hard hidden in the eyes, though, and in the set of the jaw. Like Eichmann. Like Martin Bormann. I felt bad for Pafko. The real action had been somewhere else, after all. He had gotten stuck in a nasty little Asian backwater. I was his private Guadalcanal. I was sorry, but I had done my best. So had Pafko. So had we all, even Cole, in his own way. In the final analysis, I suppose it was a fitting end for that globe-trotting Jay Gatsby.

32.
Operation Flying Dutchman

Pafko gave me the ATF version on the Hawaii leg. As far as ATF was concerned, Frank Cole was simply the world's number-one professional gun runner and dealer in murder and pirated technology. The problem was that Cole was in Libya. The trick was to lure him out. One of the longhairs in the Washington office had thought up the trick. They called it Operation Flying Dutchman.

"The key was larceny," Pafko said. "The human heart longs for nothing so much as a chance to cheat its neighbor. People will swallow almost anything that promises that chance."

"Even men like Cole?"

"Even men like Qaddafi," Pafko said. "Qaddafi was the key. We thought he would go for it, especially if the fall guys were the old colonial powers and his OPEC pals the Saudis."

"I sense a coming reference to oil," I said. I had come to distrust deals based on oil.

"Oh, yes," Pafko said. "You see Libya still owes the Italians as many lire as there are stars in the Milky Way. I don't suppose it keeps Qaddafi up at night, but it has certain inconveniences."

"How's that?"

"For one thing, angry bankers are always breathing down your neck. That makes it a nuisance to do new business. No help for it, though, if you need your entire cash flow to run World Terrorism International. He wanted to pay his debts like an honest man, but nobody had come up with a plausible way for him to do it."

"Until recently," I prompted.

"Until it occurred to our house longhair in consultation with some of the owls at DDA that he might plausibly pay off the debt in oil. That is, if the deal were arranged by an honest broker with the proper connections."

"Wouldn't that just knock down his oil revenue?"

"That was the trick. Let's say the deal was structured as half purchase and half barter. Two million barrels, just to illustrate. The price on the deal is set at thirty dollars. The Italians pay cash for half and retire thirty million of debt for the other half."

"But the spot price isn't thirty dollars," I argued. "It's heading for more like twenty dollars."

"So it is. The Italians get forty million dollars' worth of oil for thirty million, and at the same time they write off thirty million of Libyan debt. That works out to thirty-three cents on the dollar, which isn't so bad if your current expectation is zero. Of course you can jimmy the figures a little and get slightly different results."

"And what's in it for Qaddafi?"

"He comes out smelling like a rose. He gets rid of old debt so he can borrow more and go on paying for terrorism. It's easier to do business with Italians. He also gets to claim that he is sticking to the OPEC price while he exceeds his quota by the amount of his Italian debts. Actually he is discounting his price by a factor of two and overproducing like a runaway faucet, which gives it to the Saudis with a red-hot poker."

"The touch of larceny."

"The Saudis are the key. Short of shooting them all, cheating them is the thing Qaddafi likes best in life. Our longhair thought he might even spring his tame American to pull it off."

"Cole," I said.

"Who had Italian contacts going back to the OSS."

"Could a deal like this actually have gone through?"

"Not a snowball's chance. But Qaddafi doesn't know this, because it happens every hour in the Tripoli bazaar. What was supposed to happen was, Cole gets off the plane with the Libyan delegation, makes a strategic wrong turn into a narrow corridor, picks up new identity papers, and boards the next flight for Moscow. That's what Cole thinks. Before he gets on, we grab him."

"In the beginning was oil," I said. "The same was in the beginning with God."

"They haven't figured a way to charge for air,"

Pafko said. He and I had the potential of becoming friends.

"Cole must have known better than to think a cockamamy deal like this would come off," I suggested.

"It goes without saying. Cole just wanted a ticket. Tripoli was beginning to pall. Cole was ready to jump ship. The trouble was, he had to have a destination. His native land had nothing for him but prison. What Cole was persuaded to believe was that the KGB awaited with open arms and a dacha on the Black Sea. He was right. To the KGB boys, copping Cole meant instant promotion. ATF doesn't work that way."

I thought of the two men speaking in pidgin Russian. "How was this supposed to work?"

"The KGB thought they were getting a black box. You know, one of those ECM* gizmos. Our latest. It was to be delivered courtesy of Cole Export-Import. The CIA helped set it up."

"Why was the CIA supposed to be helping their ex into the hands of the KGB?"

"That part took some thinking out. You have to look at Cole's history. Cole was a loose cannon, with operations to blow from time to Timbuktu. All in all, the CIA might prefer Cole in Moscow to Cole on trial in the First Federal District. At least some CIA people might. It was like every good scam. It used Cole's trump card to trap him."

"But was it plausible? How did you get the KGB to buy in?"

"It wasn't all that hard. We almost had Cole

---

*Electronic countermeasures

twice, once in Jakarta and once in Malta. We think somebody in the old-boy network tipped him off."

"So who was the CIA liaison for this scam?"

"Fellow in the Inspector General's Office," Pafko said. "Fellow named Oren Lewes."

When they finally came through with the food, it was straight businessman's detox after a week in Asia. Beef, chicken, and rice. I remembered, the sushi was only on outgoing flights. I seemed not destined to win at certain things. Pafko ate the way government employees eat a free meal. I bought him a couple of Scotches, and say this, they at least had Glenlivet.

"What went wrong?" I probed.

"We'll have to wait for the after-action report," he said. "Fact is, we may never know."

"Your people didn't shoot him?"

"Not hardly. The triggerman jumped out into a crowd and got away. He left a Uzi with no prints. Maybe Qaddafi wised up at the last minute and sent a trigger. You can make up your own theory."

"Operation Flying Dutchman," I mused.

"We thought Operation Man Without a Country was too long," Pafko said. He sipped the Glenlivet and nodded. I had told him what single malts were and talked him out of using ice cubes. "It's a shame really. The man had a kind of genius. He was the best we ever ran up against. Absolutely the best. His technique was impeccable. Zero defects all the way. He had the requisite character, too. He was a pure technician. He was totally amoral, without any ideology or conscience. He sold weapons and technology to anybody. Anybody who could come up with cash money. After forty years in the Agency, how do you account for that?"

"He probably just considered it an extended form of free trade," I said. "He had spent a lifetime defending a bunch of nerds who didn't even understand how the world worked. In the end, he just said screw them all. It was laissez-faire. The free market. He wanted to be cut in on the action."

"And ended up under house arrest in Tripoli," Pafko said. It was getting a little philosophical for his taste. "Too bad, really. He would have made a hell of an ATF agent."

"You know what they say about cops and criminals," I needled.

Pafko ignored it. "The funny thing was that he didn't look like a criminal. He looked like, I don't know . . ."

"A suitcase carrier," I said.

We were on the runway at Honolulu. Pafko had a direct flight back, but I was stopping in Los Angeles.

"I was put on you in case you turned out to be some kind of super deep-cover CIA coverupper. They were trying to work it out why you were paying social calls on Hamer and Allbright. After the Hennessey shooting my boss had me traipse around after you in case you turned out to be part of the old-boy network. There was even a wild theory that you were a triggerman. Another theory had it that Cole had made alternative plans to make the switch in Singapore. It had a certain credibility stemming from the fact that Singapore was where he warehoused his stolen gizmos."

"Did you subscribe to this theory?"

"Not for a minute. I had a talk about you with Laura Westin. I told them their theory was idiotic, that you were a stray sheep."

"And were you ever right," I said.

"It was just God's way of keeping me from being in on the big pinch."

"Sorry," I said.

"Never mind," said Pakfo. "The guys who were there are probably getting reprimands permanent to their two-oh-ones. They think I was a prophet. The only thing they still don't quite understand is what your role in it was."

"You're telling me," I said.

I thought about it on the flight from Honolulu to Los Angeles. Long flight.

33.
Dalang

The only car in the driveway this time was a faded and beat up VW. I don't know why, but it gave me some small comfort that the Jaguar was hers. He was gardening again. What I liked about it was the way he put sections of newspaper down so he didn't get dirt on the knees. Never mind that he was only wearing old work trousers. Danauer just didn't look at things that way.

"Keith, good heavens, whatever happened to you?" He seemed genuinely concerned. Fact was, he looked worse than I did. In his case, though, the beating up was going on on the inside.

"I got mugged," I said. .

"It's Chicago," he said. "It's simply terrible. In fact, Tien felt it was an additional inducement when we got the offer."

"It was only pain," I said. "There are worse things

in life. Personally, I would rather be beaten up than go through life doubting my own judgments."

He gave me an odd look.

"But never mind that," I said. "I didn't come by to talk about that. I dropped in to talk about old times."

"Old times," Danauer said. "Why don't I make us some coffee? I haven't yet had my morning demitasse."

He made it with that same awkward precision. His coffee making had the absentminded air that masked a man who always knew exactly what he was doing. We had it in his study. Danauer sat behind his great oak desk like a teacher in front of a class of one.

"It must have been terrible for you at Heidelberg," I said. "I can imagine going through that as a young man. The world falling apart around you because the men who knew better didn't have the guts to act. Your father, your degree unfinished. You must have really learned to appreciate order. Also to value gutsy action."

"You sound as if you are going through some kind of crisis," Danauer said.

"Oh, the world is," I said. "The world is."

"Were there unusual circumstances in your mugging?"

"Less unusual than one might think," I said. "I've recently acquired a gift for empathy. I can understand, for instance, how difficult it must have been to spend one's life as a poor white of the academic profession. A great man, but always an adjunct. A visiting scholar. Often without tenure. And all because the damn Nazis interrupted your degree."

Danauer drew himself up to full lectern demeanor. His cheeks really were getting hollow, and the veins stood out in his neck. "I don't quite follow this train of conversation," he said. "My personal affairs are private."

"Oh, quite," I said. "Quite, quite."

I took a long sip of my espresso. I was watching to see how long Danauer could hold his lectern pose. It was pretty essential to the lingan-dorgan thing. He was working hard to hang on to that.

"Let's talk about forgery," I said. "I have also become very interested in forgeries."

I thought I caught a flicker. It was like a little movement of the left eyelid, a betrayal by nerves and involuntary muscle contractions and the very pulsing of blood through thin-walled capillaries. He remained at a sitting position of attention. "Forgeries?"

I told him about the Latief confession. I explained what it said and how I had come to be in possession of it. I gave a summary of the actions I had taken to check the facts. He listened intently. "How do you know it is a forgery?"

"Does it make a difference how I know?"

"Of course it does," Danauer said.

"To begin with there are the solecisms," I said. "The evolution of Bahasa was extremely rapid. The switch from Dutch to English phonetics took place within a generation. Sukarno still signed his name S-O-E. The change in Bahasa took another leap after 1965. The Latief confession is written in an idiom that did not come into being until the 1970s."

"Such matters are conjectural," Danauer argued. "No two linguists agree. Perhaps Latief merely spent an unusual amount of time with English speakers."

"Oh, he did, he did," I said. "But it's not only the words. There's the addendum. He has Sukarno meeting with Aidit when he was out on an inspection tour of Kalimantan."

"Memory is fallible." Danauer spoke in a measured voice. "Where were you yourself on a given weekend? I daresay you can't account for two of the four in any month of last summer. Napoleon's own memoirs contain errors in the order of battle."

"It's a question of the weight of the evidence," I said. "It is possible that Latief wrote very forward-looking Indonesian. It's also possible that he made more than twenty errors of memory about time and place, even though he was a lifetime counterintelligence officer. It's possible, but it's highly unlikely."

"Nevertheless, such documents remain in dispute," Danauer insisted. "Especially if there is corroborating evidence."

"Oh, there is, there is," I said. "That's the script exactly."

"I don't follow you," Danauer said.

"It's perfectly simple. A document of this sort can create an enormous mess, especially if the facts are basically true."

"You believe they are, apparently."

"Oh, they are indeed."

"Then pray tell me why," Danauer said. "Why would someone create a forged confession that told the truth?"

"The real question," I said, "is who? A prime suspect would be the discoverer. There would be plenty of doubters, especially if he could come up with only a vague explanation of how he got his hands on it. Cynical people might think he was perpetrating a hoax."

"But surely he would manage to do a better job of it."

"I'm happy you think so," I said. "I happen to think so myself. I expect an advanced graduate student might make fewer mistakes."

"Then someone in one of the intelligence agencies?" Danauer was reaching, and he knew it.

"I considered that. I turned it over a few times. The trouble is, the people who have the expertise are not in possession of the facts, and the people who know the necessary facts, Oren Lewes, for instance, lack the necessary expertise. That's why Oren keeps the lines open to old stringers like you and me, in case he needs to make an end run. I suppose he could have ordered the paper up from FE-Five as a disinformation exercise, but he would have gotten all sort of funny looks."

"Then who?" Danauer's voice and slumping posture reflected deep resignation.

"You know who," I said. "The dalang. The man who actually pulled the strings on the coup."

Danauer did his best to bristle, but he wasn't pulling it off. "It's a hell of a trick," I said. "Worthy of a great dalang. Lay a web of circumstantial evidence. Then walk your pigeon through it, handing him the bogus document in the process. When he publishes it, jump all over the little mistakes. Or better yet, leave it to the piranha school of assistant professors at Berkeley and Cornell. It's downright devilish. It squares everything forever. Never mind whose career it smashes to smithereens. Or who was already smashed in the nicest possible way by being saved from himself when he precociously worked out the truth."

"You're making wild leaps." The veins were bulging in Danauer's neck.

"You made the wild leaps," I said. "I can't tell you how I admire the pure technical brilliance."

Danauer was getting slowly to his feet. He was holding his left hand on the top of the desk to steady himself. His right hand held a Luger. It had that streamlined German look, the same as the German army helmets. It was an art-deco pistol, really. It was my personal favorite of the various types with which I was rapidly becoming acquainted.

"Please be serious," I said. "You're beginning to confuse the puppeteer and the puppets. This isn't your part of it. You're not a shooter."

"I would say you attacked me," he said.

"Horsefeathers," I said. "You're not the type who can wing it as he goes along."

I didn't really think he would shoot, but I didn't care for the way his hand was shaking. I had no idea what kind of trigger tension the Krauts like in their pistols.

"Maybe they would send me to prison, but my accomplishment would be preserved," he said.

"Accomplishment preserved," I muttered. "A statue in the Langley courtyard right next to Nathan Hale. Go ahead and shoot, you'll probably miss. What would you do with the body? Governments you can dispose of, but bodies are out of your line."

"That bastard Cole," he said. He said it with real conviction. "I never imagined he would grow into such a reprobate."

"Age does it to a man," I said. "It enables us to see people clearly as they really are."

"He was an unprincipled man," Danauer said. "They were all unprincipled men."

"But you made good use of them. You're like the woman in the story who had no need of bad qualities because she could make such good use of those who had them. But you still had a string or two to jerk. Just in case Cole got to spill the beans, you had fixed it. I guess it was Oren who finally took care of the Cole problem."

"Bastards," he said again. "So what are you going to do about it?"

"My duty as a scholar and a citizen," I said. "A seeker and illuminator of truth."

"And what will that prove?"

"The world will know the truth."

"To what good purpose?"

"So ordinary people can make an informed decision about their future. Through democratic process. In full knowledge of the true past." Even as I spoke, I had the old uneasy sensation that Danauer was getting the best of me.

"No one will believe you," Danauer said. "It will be one more tall tale about what *might* have happened in 1965. A novel. Worse yet, half of them will believe you. The bad half. They will use what you write and make a grand shit mess of everything. You will have helped the bad guys to triumph in the Cold War."

"We'll see," I said.

"You'll see," he said. "I have lung cancer. The doctors say I'll be dead in six months. If I don't shoot myself the minute you pull out of the driveway."

"That's a shame about the cancer," I said. "If you decide to shoot yourself, the proper technique is to place the pistol in the back of your mouth elevated at a forty-five-degree angle. You hold the butt with both hands and pull the trigger with your thumbs."

I met Tien Danauer coming up the walk with a bag of groceries. I glanced at my car blocking her driveway and gave a little shrug of apology. She gave me a big smile. I smiled back. I didn't know what else to do. She didn't seem to notice the facial contusions. I was smiling, but inside I was angry and confused. There just didn't seem to be a right way to feel about things. The hell of it was that Danauer was right. When all was said and done, he was still my old teacher, whatever he had done. When all was said and done, I still felt that on the whole it would be better if our side won the Cold War, or at least managed not to lose it too badly.

34.
Cowboys

On the red-eye back to Chicago I put together a précis of what a really informed article might say about the coup. The preamble might say that it was one of the last bits of melodramatic world fixing that the intelligence cowboys engaged in through the 1950s and '60s. Frank Cole had been the action officer on the scene. Oren Lewes in Saigon had managed to juggle resources to provide backup. Danauer, the ivory-tower intellectual, had been the brains behind it.

It was cheap at twice the price. Lewes gave Cole the means to persuade the Indonesian generals of CIA support. Cole used Dalippah, the woman he shared with Sukarno, to provide the president with advance warning, while a cagey Indonesian general used a schizo counterintelligence officer named Latief to provide Sukarno with independent confirmation.

Sukarno had no choice but to act, and to take the Communists along with him.

If he didn't move, the generals would throw him out. He needed foot troops, so he pulled in Aidit and Communist officers like the air force chief of staff. They chose a young colonel named Untung as their front man in case it fouled up. As it did. The coup never had a chance. None at all. Sukarno walked straight into the trap, and the jaws of the crocodile closed over him.

That was about what an article would say, or an after-action report, for that matter, although I was pretty sure that none existed. Not at Langley, at any rate. That wasn't the way these men operated. A wink, a nod, a theoretical conversation. That was how they would have put it together, in Teddy's, in Santa Monica, at drinking spots on Tu Do Street. With nothing on paper, and barring a live confession, which was rather unlikely, there could never be an article. It would remain exactly what Danauer had said it was: another clever fiction.

The cute part, really, was where I had come in. I had presented a minor problem in grad school, when I wrote a paper that might have focused more attention than the boys were prepared to deal with. Danauer dealt with that. Oh, how he dealt with it. The second time I presented a problem, by publishing the paper, it proved to be fortuitous.

By then Cole had gone bad and become a problem himself. That was the trouble with those cowboy cabals. He had taken to blackmailing the other conspirators. If they didn't cover for him, help him snitch secret technology and peddle munitions to Qaddafi, he would blow the whistle on the whole thing. It must have presented a terrible dilemma to Danauer and Lewes, especially when the Treasury boys got on to him.

That's where I came back in. That's what accounted for the two peculiar mandalas. My article presented them with the perfect fix.

Cole had a habit of using businessmen as his couriers, first a reluctant oil engineer named Leitsey, then a less reluctant one named Marlon Crockett. Crockett had provided a channel to the Sumatra strike force, and then had stuck around as an occasional CIA retainer. He had made good use of privileged information.

Cole had also used Dalippah's nephew, a young economics student named Moko, to put together his street troops. Crockett and Moko had been drawn into a mutually profitable relationship. It was particularly useful when the time came to get the spurious Latief confession into my hands.

It was beautiful, really. The perfect cover-up. Why not, Danauer must have suggested, expose the entire operation, only in such a way that the exposé would be discredited forever. I was a perfect patsy. It didn't hurt to put in the fix so the academic world already thought of me as a crackpot. Anything I wrote would be dismissed as paranoid delusion. I even had doubts about myself. And if Cole ever got into position to sing, he would just be quoting the theory of a crackpot professor.

It was all very neat. Only somewhere the Cole side got wind of it and tried to find out exactly what I was on to, and had to be prevented in turn, which was why, in the end, I was guarded as by eyes that watch lest a sparrow fall. Hamer, Allbright, Gus Friedler, and poor Max were all less fortunate. I would always miss Max.

That was about where I had gotten to when the wheels of the plane hit O'Hare #1. It was too late to catch Westin so I called to tell her I was okay and checked into a hotel. I was tired and drained and was going to have no trouble sleeping during the day. But I also felt a certain perverse satisfaction. I had gotten to the scholar's ultimate destination. I knew the truth. The essential truth anyway. At least I intended to present it that way to Sorel and Laura Westin.

35.
Squid Pud Prik

Our cabal held its after-action review not at Perroquet but at Thai Little Home Café, which is pretty far north on Kedzie. It is run by one of those families of Asian immigrants who are making it so hard for the kids of WASP lawyers and Jewish doctors to get into Harvard anymore. I was trying to get Westin acclimated to peppers and coriander.

"So that's why Indoil started moving up back in December," Westin said. It was on her mind because Indoil had capitulated that very morning. Crockett's tender was over the top.

"September, not December," I corrected.

"It was all in the charts," Sorel said. "Not that inside information isn't better than fine gold. Gold is looking weak to me, in fact."

"Was Cole selling stuff to the Russians when he

was still on the Tech Systems board?" Westin wanted to know.

"Pafko wasn't sure," I said. "They think his liaison work may have given him the idea."

Westin thought Cole was fascinating. "But what I don't understand is why he didn't just stay in Libya."

"Maybe it was those veils the women wear," I said. "There is also some evidence that he had begun to wear out his welcome with the good colonel. There was a matter of some dud fuses. Just one of those things, but he couldn't get Qaddafi to understand how things could go wrong in a capitalist transaction. Qaddafi also couldn't understand why Cole couldn't lay hands on a stray hydrogen bomb, or at least a couple of Redeye missiles."

"That Tech Systems is a hell of a little outfit," Sorel said. "The chart says that it's about to take off like a rocket."

We were done with a red-hot dish of shrimp soup, and they were bringing out yum nua and squid pud prik. I reassured Westin that the active ingredient word was squid.

"So who were the people who picked you up at the Jakarta Mandarin? I don't quite see how they could get a bunch of Islamic terrorists to join in the plot." Sorel was genuinely perplexed.

"Those must have been Moko's men, silly," Westin said. She thought Sorel was amazingly slow on the uptake about certain things. "I'm afraid you're not going to be able to justify quite all your travel on the SEAAAC grant. They called today to query the first set of vouchers."

"And how about the people who came to

straighten up at the safe house?" Sorel wondered. "Were they KGB?"

"I've wondered about that myself," I said. "Was Lewes in such a box that the only manpower he could command were the Russians he was supposedly shipping Cole to? I suppose I could try to find out, but it doesn't seem important somehow."

"The important thing is living to tell the tale," Sorel said. "Cut your losses, as they say, live to trade another day. You're okay, now? No internal injuries? No post-trauma nightmares?"

"Just sex dreams," I said. "I expect I'll be ready for a night's sleep. By Monday all that will be left of the shiner is an involuntary wink for a girl in the front row."

"So the whole thing was just to have it squared if Cole got to Moscow or First District Court and started singing his head off."

"Or some bright young graduate student put two and two together and grew up to publish a paper."

"Then who shot him? The Libyans or the CIA?"

"Take your pick," I said. "Maybe Lewes found a way to tip off the Libyans."

Thai desserts aren't particularly recommended so we cleaned up the last of the pud Thai and washed it down with the last of the draft beer. I was fading fast. Sorel sat shaking his head at the wonder of it.

"We sure cleaned up on it," he finally said. He had made just over $22,000 on his Tidelands shorts, and I shudder to think how much on Indoil calls.

"Who was this Siti person?" Westin said.

I treated it as a rhetorical question. I ignored her resolutely. Sorel called for the bill, which came to just under thirty bucks, and when he reached for his wallet neither of us budged an inch.

"Just one other thing," Westin said. "When they ransacked your house, what were Cole's men looking for?"

I opened my mouth to answer, but it was only a professor's reflex. She just didn't stop catching me off guard.

"The Latief papers?" I tried.

"But if it was the Latief thing, I don't see how Cole's people knew to look. How could they have known about that? And the Lewes people already knew exactly what was in it. They had their own copy," she reasoned slowly. "So why did they tear your house apart? Or rather who?"

That was the trouble with talking to Laura Westin. Who indeed? And just when I had every prospect of a solid night's sleep. It started to bother me on the separate taxi ride I had to take to conceal from Sorel my residence at Westin's apartment. I was about at the point of breaking down and soliciting her opinion, but she greeted me at the door with the announcement that the dean had left a message on her call box. He had called on the off chance that she might be up to date on my whereabouts. A Professor Emeritus B. H. Frazier from Los Angeles was trying to get in touch with me urgently.

36.
The Stochastic Man

There is just no delicate way of breaking the news about a suicide. It didn't make it any easier that I couldn't recall knowing any B. H. Fraziers. He had to remind me in the elliptical manner of the self-absorbed old that he had once served on my doctoral committee. That must have been where he met Danauer, he thought. He remembered me for the difficulties I had with statistical methods, but he had been assured by Danauer that I was sound in my own field. It was a stochastic principle of his, he said, to accept the otherwise unsupported opinion of a reliable authority. He was pleased that my subsequent success had borne out his judgment. He himself had been enticed to spend his declining years in Westwood by a combination of financial inducement and the California weather.

He had turned into rather a hermit, alone as he

so often was in his Westwood flat. That was the trouble with changing cities late in life, although he couldn't say that he much minded. Oh, he swam every day, thank you, and taught his single class (on yearly extension from the board of regents, witnessing the steady and alarming decline in the study and *teaching* of statistics), and he managed to keep himself quite busy following the interest rates on his jumbo CDs and tracking the switch fund where he kept the variable portion of his private retirement funds. He even went to Dodger Stadium occasionally, baseball being a statistician's game, really. He had a sort of sixth sense for when Valenzuela was going to have a bad outing, and he didn't doubt that his feeling for numbers had something to do with it. And every now and then he was called in to backstop the computer whiz kids at Santa Monica Institute, who could do just about anything but basic arithmetic.

Come to think of it, that was how he had run across Danauer again, who in his own way had turned into a hermit too. He had invited old Fred to join him one day when the Cubs were in town, God knew why he chose the Cubs, and rather to his surprise Fred had accepted. They had cheered both teams indiscriminately, and settled for a single beer and hot dog, so that Fred had ended up inviting him back for an Indonesian dinner. Tien had done magnificently, magnificently on the spur of the moment.

After that they had seen each other every week or so, this season sitting directly behind Jack Nicholson at the Coliseum when, he thought it was the Bullets, were in town. He had only been invited back for dinner a couple of times. In fact, he thought Fred rather liked to get out of the house, or perhaps Fred just liked the Lakers. Now the Lakers were a little glitzy for *his* taste, but they could both relate to a man like Kareem, forty-one, goggled, and still an MVP in spite of the baldness he wore with rather moving honesty. In fact, it was a date for the Trail-blazer game that he had been calling Fred about.

You never really knew another person, that was one of the things he had come to learn. Behind that quiet Oriental facade, Tien had proved remarkably resilient and quite competent when it came to making arrangements. Still, it must have been an ordeal for the poor thing. Hardly a friend in the world, still a veritable war bride after twenty years, she hadn't known anyone to call—not even the *L.A. Times* to see to a proper obituary. He had even wondered for a moment whether she would have thought to call *him*. That Oriental inwardness, he supposed, which in the West was so easily taken as the absence of emotion.

He would have expected to find a few of Fred's old cronies—in Irvine, or certainly at Pasadena—but he had reckoned without the fracturing force of the years. I was the only one he could find. Otherwise he would not have thought of asking me to come. Tien herself had been adamant in opposition, but he had decided to call on his own initiative. A person who could keep all those S-U names straight, there couldn't have been too many of us. The truth was, it would have meant a lot to Fred. He often spoke of me, a kind of concern in his voice, as of a son who had moved far away. "He had terminal cancer, you probably didn't know," Frazier concluded.

"Exactly when did he shoot himself?" I asked.

"Shoot himself? Oh, yes, I see what you mean. It was last evening. But he didn't shoot himself, you know. He took pills."

37.
Prime Mover

It was a grim, private little ceremony, something like
a Justice of the Peace wedding with Tien and Frazier
and Mr. Harmon of Harmon Memorial Services (Spe-
cialists in Direct Burial, Immediate Cremation, Gifts
to Science—Licensed Professional Staff) presiding.
I was cast as best man. I knew academic contract
people didn't get flyovers or rifle volleys, but it still
felt a little understated. Tien had chosen Immediate
Cremation, rather over Frazier's dissent, I gathered.
Danauer had never expressed an opinion on the subject, but she thought it was consistent with his personal philosophy. She was holding up well. It was
Frazier who looked as if he might throw himself on
the pyre.

When Mr. Harmon was done propitiating the
gods of secular modernity, Frazier drove us back to

the Danauer bungalow. Tien had seemed a little hesitant about inviting us back, as if unsure about the customs of this distant American tribe, and I couldn't help wondering what she would think if she knew Frazier had gotten me aside to ask, "I say, after a proper interval, what do you suppose the poor thing would say if I proposed marriage?" She looked as if she hardly knew what to do with the two of us for an hour of tea and commiseration. In fact, I seemed to be the primary focus of her attention, and Frazier, looking a little hurt but sensitive to her feelings, took both the cue and his leave in short order.

Alone with her in the house, I realized that the thing I had not quite noticed before was its impersonality. Oh, there were a few of the carvings and wall hangings and masks that an Asianist picks up, but nothing that would not have been selected by a casual traveler. Danauer evidently had not cared much for personal possessions—just the one rare gem that he had acquired in middle life. She stood uneasily in the middle of the living room as if again uncertain of Western customs. I let myself settle into a California rattan chair.

"Will you keep the house?"

"I beg your pardon?" she said distractedly.

"I mean, I wasn't sure if the Institute leased or sold outright."

"Yes, I see," she said. "I haven't decided yet."

She seemed to be straining to remember something. "Will you have a drink?" she finally said.

"No thanks."

"Coffee then?"

I started to say no, then remembered Danauer at the grinder. It would give her something to do.

"Coffee would be very nice."

While she made the coffee, I got up for a last glance at Danauer's library. I am an inveterate inspector of bookshelves. I used to fancy that I could read human character in the selection of books. Danauer had the expected collection of academic works in English, German, Dutch, and a half-dozen Asian languages. There were few novels, and none at all from recent years, but there was a complete collection of *Reader's Digest* Condensed Books going back to 1950. It was a commentary on something, I couldn't quite say what. On the way back I glanced idly in the direction of the Danauers' bedroom. It was an idle impulse, honestly, done without any intention of prying. Theirs was a standard American middle-class bedroom with a double bed covered by an afghan, crocheted not in the country of its name but in the spirit of pioneer grandmothers. I was wondering if Tien had done it herself when I saw the suitcase.

It was hidden in the closet, but a corner was reflected by the full-length mirror on the closet door. I still had no intention of snooping, but I just had to be sure. It was in there all right, a single nondescript worn plaid bag, and on top of it was an American passport and a ticket to Singapore in the name of T. Danauer.

"Frederick would have liked you to have his books," her voice wafted in from the kitchen.

I closed the ticket envelope and flipped it back

onto the passport. I made it back to the rattan chair just as the smell of fresh espresso preceded Tien into the living room.

"Will you stay in Santa Monica then?"

"I imagine so," she said. "Cream and sugar?"

I nodded. She poured the coffee from an unbreakable plastic pot into an unchippable plastic mug. A Danish designer had wracked his brain for three or four nanoseconds over their design. I had to stop her from heaping in sugar with the Asian relish for condiments.

"No note, no will. It's strange," I said.

"There is a will." She appeared tense and distracted. "There will be a formal reading, I believe. He was ill, you know."

She excused herself as I braced for the rush of the espresso. Why did we do these things to ourselves? A friend once explained to me that chicory originated as a wartime supplement. The coffee companies retained it because people had become habituated to the bitter taste. I took the shock of bitterness in a single large gulp. Tien was standing in the doorway with the Luger pointed at my midsection.

"Not again," I said.

She walked cautiously in my direction, holding the pistol in a firm interlocking grip.

"Be careful with that thing," I urged.

I was calculating furiously, but as Frazier said, I have never been very good at calculations. Who was Tien Danauer, really, and how much chance did I have of tipping the table, pulling the rug, and flinging the pot of coffee in her face? I was doing other calculations too.

"You sent the men to my house," I said. "Danauer kept it a secret from you. He was beginning to suspect."

She made a small adjustment in her aim. She didn't speak. I realized how little she had spoken in all the times I had been with them.

"So was it the Russians or the Chinese? Or somebody else?"

My own money would have been on the Russians. The men who came to the safe house had spoken in English and Russian. Not that it proved anything. I was beginning to learn that nothing in the shadow world was quite what it seemed.

Of one thing there was no doubt: After a dozen cowboys and amateurs, I had finally run up against a professional. Her two-fisted grip was pure understated Dirty Harry, and her hands didn't shake. She had measured the range of the pistol against the range of the coffeepot and was closing the distance deliberately. I hadn't been sure about Danauer, but I had no doubt that she would shoot. I also had few doubts that she would hit her target. For a moment I thought that she was measuring the optimal range, but she was only maneuvering to get a better view of the contents of my coffee mug.

"Oh, no," I said. I felt a familiar leap in my heart rate.

"You won't die," she said. "You have a strong young heart. Just don't have a second cup."

A wave of nausea began to surge upward from

some neglected internal region in the vicinity of my pancreas.

"Drink water when you come around," she said. "You won't require medical attention."

"Men seldom use pills," I said with bemused realization. Even from a great distance I noted the slurring of my own speech. "Men use a gun, if one is available."

"Lock the door on the way out," she said. "I would have locked it. Lose the key."

When I came around, it was just as she said. I drank several glasses of water, then washed the glass and left it on the drying rack where she had left the coffeepot and mug. Outside her kitchen window a slender crescent of moon hung over the Pacific night.

The clock above the sink revealed that it was almost three A.M. I had another red-eye flight to catch. There would be plenty of time to philosophize about it all later. It had happened, was all. There were actions I could theoretically take, but by now the dragon lady would be about six hours out of Singapore. They could always turn the plane around, but I couldn't quite fancy their waking the head of the National Security Council at four o'clock in the morning on the word of an obviously groggy and undoubtedly half-cracked professor.

Which must have been the reason she left me alive. On the whole it was tighter and more convenient. Dead, I was an additional loose end. Alive, I had no story to tell without serious personal inconvenience. It made me queasy again to think how quickly and accurately she had thought the situation through.

Of course, there might have been an element of charity. After all, I had flown two thousand miles to stand beside her at the burial of her husband. She might have been moved by a reciprocal kind thought. She might have been, but I doubted it.

This new reality was going to take some getting used to, and I wasn't being helped along in my analysis by the double Excedrin headache she had failed to mention. I thought of all the years she had lived as Danauer's wife. I couldn't help wondering whether, in all those years, there had ever been a moment of true feeling? It was a staggering thought, but I have been told that it happens in marriages where neither partner is a secret agent. How many years had it been? Twenty, Frazier had said. Seventeen or eighteen at least. What could you pay a person for service like that? What kind of loyalty inspired it? What goal provided the justification? My mind boggled at the thought, but then little men were inside there pounding away with miniature jackhammers.

There were answers, all right, but in a few hours they would step off a plane in Singapore, change documents, and merge forever into the great faceless mass of the Third World. There was nothing I could do about it. Somewhere a reception awaited, a quiet drink, a medal pinned on in secret. Somewhere a master dalang awaited his master operative. The identity of the dalang—his country and his cause— was the final piece of the puzzle I would never possess. That was the condition for my staying alive. It was forever consigned to Max's unexplained 41 percent.

It was like those airtight medieval proofs of God. When you were finished, all you had done was move the mysterious part one step farther back. The Prime Mover was out there—in Peking or Moscow, or in a dark-horse contender like Jakarta or Damascus or Tripoli—but He was forever Unknown and Unknowable. It was one more crocodile story, and its final moral, as Sorel would say, was getting out alive.

I thought briefly of having a go at Danauer's books and papers, but they would have been thoroughly sanitized by skilled and knowledgeable hands. Like Max, Danauer may have had intimations of his fate, but unlike Max he had gone down to sheol without a friend for whom to leave a last message. There was nothing left to do but get into my rental car and drive away.

38.
Loose End

What the whole thing taught you was something about the nature of sleep. It takes insomnia to teach you about sleep. Sleep is the poor man's Zen. You can't make it happen. You let it happen.

The SEAAAC people finally agreed to pop for half the travel vouchers, which was more than I had any reason to hope for. I made a little better than $4,000 shorting Tidelands. House repairs weren't quite as bad as I had feared, but they were substantial. Crockett came through with his check in good order. (I have noticed that white-collar criminals are scrupulous about paying small bills.) When all was totted up, I was $757 ahead for my trouble, if you don't count the $179 I dropped at Sorel's poker game.

On the way back from Santa Monica I took a side trip to San Francisco and popped in on the Liebermans, spur of the moment ready or not. Helen thought I looked a little tired, but she didn't seem to mind and kept refilling my Laphroaig and urging me to stay over. Jeremy seemed to be coming into his own. He had gained a couple of pounds already, and his color looked a lot better. He was quite interested in the details of my travels. Helen had discovered the kris, of course, but before she could start in, he told her that he had gotten it years ago for his birthday, and she had no choice but to accept the story. I think he was most proud of his own skill as a liar and the little touch of embroidery, but I could tell that I had risen a small notch in his estimation. I had provided the basic concept of his cover story. Say what you will, when all is said and done, there is nothing we so greatly admire as the finely modulated criminal mind.

Appendix A

September 30, 1965

The six murdered generals were Army Chief of Staff Achmed Yani and Generals Parman, Panjaitan, Hartono, Soeprapto, and Soetojo. Yani, Panjaitan, and Hartono were actually shot at their homes while resisting the kidnappers (Yani in front of his eleven-year-old son) and were probably dead by the time the vans arrived at Halim. A seventh general, Defense Minister Abdul Haris Nasution, was on the list for assassination, but escaped by vaulting over the wall to the compound of the Iraqi ambassador. Nasution's three-year-old daughter received a mortal gunshot wound in the skirmish, and the kidnappers took his adjutant, Lieutenant Pierre Tendean, in the confusion of the moment. Tendean apparently resembled Nasution in the dark.

The Nasution mixup was to play a role in interpretations of the coup. In the early hours after the takeover, Radio Peking announced that *seven* generals had been murdered. The same announcement was made, in similar language, by the Communist mayor of Solo, in Central Java. To anyone with an intelligence background, the announcements provided a suggestion of Chinese foreknowledge and involvement.

Theories of the coup divide around whether the primary instigator of the movement was President Sukarno or Communist Party Chief Aidit. Untung is universally dismissed as a pawn and a lightweight, although the Cornell Paper at first tried to argue that the coup was in fact what it claimed to be, a rebellion by young officers of the Diponegoro division who were fed up by the corruption of the "Menteng" generals. Menteng is an affluent suburb of Jakarta.

The theory that Sukarno himself orchestrated the coup has intuitive appeal. He was in unique position to pull the strings. He also had great popular following among the masses, but no real political organization. Thus he needed the PKI. A Dutch journalist named Dake advanced the Sukarno thesis, citing a confession by an aide named Bambang Widjanarko, which other scholars consider dubious. An alternative version of the thesis has it that Sukarno, far from seeking personal power, was in failing health and saw the coup as the means for making Aidit or Subandrio his successor.

Scholars who blame the Communists are also split between those who see it as meddling by Peking and those who regard it as a local power play by Aidit. Aidit was a figure of some stature, having extended the Maoist canon by his theory that the Third World was an international proletariat destined to engulf the urban West. Both camps of scholars are subdivided between those who see the Communist initiative as an offensive move completing a grab for power and those who see it as a last-ditch effort to avoid annihilation by the army.

A very few scholars take at face value Untung's assertion that he acted to forestall a coup planned by the generals themselves for Armed Forces Day, November 5. In fact, the November 5 celebration turned into a day of burial and mourning for the exhumed bodies of the generals and Nasution's daughter. At the mass funeral the assembled military leaders passed the word *sikat*, or "sweep," meaning that they intended to make a clean sweep of the PKI.

The theory of an aborted military coup seems just barely possible, although the casual security at the homes of the generals makes it appear unlikely. The Indonesian Army was generally Russian-equipped, but its officers were American-trained. Yani, among others, had been treated to the Sex and Entertainment tour for senior foreign officers at Leavenworth Staff College, and the American ambassador had made a personal plea to President Johnson not to cut off funding of a sophisticated communications system which was particularly dear to Yani.

The argument that Suharto himself orchestrated the coup was put forward by a scholar named Wertheim in *Pacific Affairs*. About all that could be cited in its favor was the cui bono argument: Who ultimately profited? Suharto claimed to have first heard of the coup when a neighbor woke him to say there was gunfire down the block.

My article ("The Pluto Thesis: Proposal for the Existence of an Unaccounted Player in the Indonesian Coup of 1965," *Pacifica* XXIII, pp. 1–19) was in fact an annotated survey of the various other theories. It argued that each theory of the coup might well have some validity, but only as a portion of an uncompleted overall picture. It proposed the existence of an additional player in the events of 1965, invisible to direct sight but observable through the otherwise contradictory and irrational actions of the other players, much as the planet Pluto was first discovered by astronomers who noted orbital irregularities in the other outer planets.

Appendix B

The conspirators all met unhappy fates. Air Force Chief of Staff Dhani fled Halim in his private plane, but was eventually captured and sentenced to death for treason. Untung was captured as he stepped aboard a bus bearing an advertisement with his own name, which is Bahasa for "lucky." He was shot by firing squad. Subandrio was exiled to an island prison. In the sweep that followed, every member of the PKI Central Committee was killed save one man who happened to be in Peking. Aidit was captured in central Java and executed on the spot, after allegedly writing a confession that eventually turned up in Tokyo newspapers. Sukarno, who as Third World spokesman had been the bane of John Foster Dulles, died under house arrest.

It was Suharto who, in the early hours after the coup, thought to call the conspirators by the acronym GESTAPU. It was a brilliant piece of PR, so much so that journalistic wags observed that Untung's big mistake was in not calling his group the First October Movement. Suharto gradually consolidated power, first seeking out a *dukur* who confirmed that, yes, he Suharto was destined to be the next leader. Suharto also took pains to obtain a sacred ceremonial kris that was said always to gravitate into the hands of the legitimate ruler. Persons knowledgeable in the wayang said it had all been predestined. It is a fact known to every Indonesian schoolchild that in the Bharata Yudda, the great final battle of the Mahabharata, the Heroes of the Right prevail in a great slaughter over the Heroes of the Left.

Appendix C

McCallum, K. A. *Oil and Mineral Policy in Indonesia, 1949–1962* (New York: Oxford, 1975).

———. *The Politics of Tin: The Malaysian Planners, the Marketplace, and the Cartel* (New York: Oxford, 1978).

Appendix D

The Central Intelligence Agency is organized differently from many of its European counterparts. Because it came into being at a late moment in American history, to meet the specific needs of the Cold War, it combines the functions of espionage, counterespionage, and covert action, which governments often separate. The primary division is between DDA (Deputy Directorate for Analysis) and DDO (Deputy Directorate for Operations, formerly DDP, or Deputy Directorate for Plans). The DDA is responsible for academic research as well as such technical work as the analysis of electronic intelligence and satellite reconnaissance. The DDO is responsible for human intelligence (HUMINT in the jargon, or the running of agents). It is also the administrative rubric for the loosely structured elements involved in covert action.

Appendix E

Price and volume charts record the movements of a stock or commodity with the use of two variables, price as measured against time (with a corollary record of time-segmented trading volume) in contrast to point and figure charts, which are concerned with price changes only and focus not on volume but on reversals, and especially on moves of a certain dimension, which are called key reversals. Advocates of price and volume charting believe that all obtainable information is already reflected in the price of a commodity or financial asset, and that one can best predict future price movements by determining whether increments in price are reinforced by increments in time-segmented volume.

Appendix F

A call option is the right to buy at a specified price within a specified amount of time (a put option being, conversely, the right to sell). Options are traded in series with various expiration dates, normally at three-month intervals, and various "strike" prices. If the underlying stock increases dramatically in excess of the strike price, the call buyer stands to make a large profit.

Let's say, for instance, that with IBM stock selling at 120 one buys the June 130 strike at 2 ($200). If, by the third Friday in June, IBM does not trade above the 130 strike, the option expires worthless and the buyer is out his $200 speculation. If, however, IBM trades above 130, the option buyer may exercise his right to purchase at 130 and sell his shares on the market at the higher price. At 132 the call buyer breaks even. At 135 he makes a $300 profit. At 140 he makes $800. At 150 he makes $1,800 per call purchased. For a speculator with good information or insight into the price movement of a particular stock, a call option presents an opportunity to get tremendous leverage for his speculative capital.

CRITIC'S CHOICE
Espionage and Suspense Thrillers

THE FORTRESS AT ONE DALLAS CENTER
  by Ron Lawrence $3.50
FATAL MEMORY by Bruce Forester $3.95
A FIST FULL OF EGO by Bruce Topol $3.75
THE PALACE OF ENCHANTMENTS
  by Hurd & Lamport $3.95
THE PANAMA PARADOX by Michael Wolfe $3.50
THE CHINESE FIRE DRILL by Michael Wolfe $2.95
THE VON KESSEL DOSSIER by Leon LeGrande $3.95
CARTER'S CASTLE by Wilbur Wright $3.95
DANGEROUS GAMES by Louis Schreiber $3.95
SHADOW CABINET by W.T. Tyler $3.95
DOUBLE TAKE by Gregory Dowling $2.95
STRYKER'S KINGDOM by W.A. Harbinson $3.95
THE HAWTHORN CONSPIRACY by Stephen Hesla $3.95
THE CORSICAN by Bill Ballinger $3.95
AMBLER by Fred Halliday $3.50
BLUE FLAME by Joseph Gilmore $3.75
THE DEVIL'S VOYAGE by Jack Chalker $3.75

Write for a free catalog at the above address.

CRITIC'S CHOICE
The greatest mysteries being published today

CAPTURED by Michael Serrian	$3.95
THE ZARAHEMLA VISION by Gary Stewart	$3.50
THE TENTH VIRGIN by Gary Stewart	$3.50
ACADEMIC MURDER by Dorsey Fiske	$3.50
DEATH OF A RENAISSANCE MAN by Linda Uccello	$3.50
A TIME TO REAP by Michael T. Hinkemeyer	$2.95
FOURTH DOWN, DEATH by Michael T. Hinkemeyer	$3.50
THE KING EDWARD PLOT by Robert Lee Hall	$3.50
ONE-EYED MERCHANTS by Kathleen Timms	$2.95
HIS LORDSHIP'S ARSENAL by Christopher Moore	$2.95
PORTRAIT IN SHADOWS by John Wainwright	$3.50
THE THIRD BLONDE by M.S. Craig	$2.95
GILLIAN'S CHAIN by M.S. Craig	$2.95
TO PLAY THE FOX by M.S. Craig	$2.95
NEW YEAR RESOLUTION by Alison Cairns	$2.95
STRAINED RELATIONS by Alison Cairns	$2.95
A CHARMED DEATH by Miles Tripp	$2.95
DEATH ON CALL by Sandra Wilkinson	$2.95
MAGGIE by Jennie Tremain	$2.95
THOSE DARK EYES by E.M. Brez	$2.95
SOMEONE ELSE'S GRAVE by Alison Smith	$2.95
THE DOWN EAST MURDERS by J.S. Borthwick	$3.50
THE GLORY HOLE MURDERS by Tony Fennelly	$2.95
MACE by James Grant	$2.95
INTIMATE KILL by Margaret Yorke	$2.95

Please send your check or money order (no cash) to:

Critic's Choice Paperbacks
31 East 28th Street
New York, N. Y. 10016

Please include $1.00 for the first book and 50¢ for each additional book to cover the cost of postage and handling.

Name _____

Street Address _____

City _____ State _____ Zip Code _____

Write for a free catalog at the above address.